It was just after two in the afternoon when we pulled up. Tim said that's the time it was always slow in the bank, specially on Thursdays.

Virgil had a double-barreled sawed-off. Those are good for scaring people, Tim said. Much better than a pistol. Virgil carried the shotgun under his coat, against his chest, held there by a loop of rawhide around his neck. Tim had a pair of pistols, like he always used to carry.

"Five minutes, Eddie," Tim said to me. Then him and Virgil went into the bank.

The clock on the dashboard was one of those digital ones. It said 2:09.

The clock said 2:12 when I heard the crack of a pistol. Then the boom of Virgil's shotgun.

People started screaming.

THE
GETAWAY MAN

THE
GETAWAY MAN

ANDREW VACHSS

VINTAGE CRIME / BLACK LIZARD
Vintage Books   A Division of Random House, Inc.   New York

A Vintage Crime/Black Lizard Original, February 2003

Library of Congress Cataloging-in-Publication Data
Vachss, Andrew H.
The getaway man / Andrew Vachss.
p.   cm.—(Vintage crime/Black Lizard)
ISBN 1-4000-3119-2 (trade paper)
1. Criminals—Fiction.   I. Title.   II. Series.
PS3572.A33 G48   2002
813'.54—dc21   2002028885

www.vintagebooks.com

Printed in the United States of America
10   9   8   7   6   5   4   3   2   1

for . . .

Cammi, Jessie Lee, Johnny the Gambler, Detroit B., Bust-Out Victor, Iberus, J.R., Everett, Water Street, the East Gary Express, the Uptown Community Organization, a whole lot of back roads, and some wrong turns.

and for . . .

Jim Procter, who drove the car.

ACKNOWLEDGMENT

Joe R. Lansdale
It's true, bro. We would have been kings.

THE
GETAWAY MAN

*E*very outfit needs a getaway man. It doesn't matter how smooth the job goes; if you don't get away with the money, it was all for nothing.

I learned that when I was just a kid, when I first started getting locked up. Once that happens the first time, it's like that's your destiny. They let you out, but they know you're coming back, and you do, too.

Inside, some guys get tattoos, so that when they get out, other guys will know where they've been. I never wanted one. I figured people can always tell, anyway.

Every time they sent me to the kiddie camps, it was for stealing cars. I never stole cars to keep; I just wanted to drive them. I wanted to learn how to do that more than anything. The only reason I took the cars was so I could practice.

When you're in one of those places for kids, guys always ask you what you're in for. The first time I went in, before I learned, I told them the truth.

I found out quick how dumb that was. When I told other guys, that first time, why I took the cars, they said that wasn't even stealing, it was just joyriding. That's what a kid does with a car, joyriding. A man wouldn't do that.

It sounds weird, but the worst thing you can be in the kiddie camps is what they call a "kid." The word means something different in there. Something very bad.

Right after I told the truth that first time, I had to fight a lot. So I wouldn't get taken for a kid.

By the next time I went in, I was smarter. I knew nobody

would understand if I told them I took the cars so I could practice my driving. So, after that, when they asked me, I always said, "Grand Theft Auto." I wasn't some little joy-rider; I was a thief.

A thief steals cars to keep. To sell, I mean. The really good thieves, they get a reputation, and people hire them to steal certain cars. Like ordering food in a restaurant, and the parking lot is the menu.

It's good to be known as a thief when you go Inside. It's even better to be known as a killer, but only a certain kind. Like if you killed someone in a fight, that would be good. Or if someone paid you to do it.

It's pretty unusual, to be in one of the kiddie places for a killing like that, but I know one guy, Tyree, who was. A drug dealer paid Tyree to shoot someone, and he did it. Everyone respected him for doing that. It was something a big-time criminal would do.

But not every killing got you respect. The sick-in-the-head kids, they were nothings. Nobody was afraid of them. Like the one who chopped up his mother with an ax. Or the one who went to school with a rifle, and shot a bunch of other kids who were bullying him.

After that kid got locked up, he still got bullied, only much worse. The kind of bullying they do in here.

Sometimes, a killing happens right where they have us locked up. The one I most remember, it was a little kid who did it. Devon, his name was. A bigger kid, Rock, had done something to him.

After Rock did what he did, he told everyone that Devon was *his* kid.

Everybody knew what had happened, but nobody said anything, even the ones who weren't scared of Rock.

After Devon got out of the infirmary, he got a shank—
that's a piece of metal you sharpen into a knife. One day, he
came up behind Rock in the cafeteria and stabbed him in
the neck. Everybody saw it.

We knew Devon had stuck him good, because they
didn't send Rock to the infirmary—they called for an
ambulance.

The guards charged in and locked us all down, so we
couldn't see what happened after that. But, later, we heard
that Rock died before the ambulance came.

If they had let Devon stay in there with us, he would
have been all right after that. Nobody would have tried to
do anything to him anymore, even with him being so little.
But they took him away, to the prison for grownups.

I didn't actually know Devon. Just his name. But I
hoped, wherever they sent him, he found another shank
real quick.

I always wanted to be a driver. It was just something that
called to me. Even when I was practicing to be good at it,
I wasn't sure where it would end. But I knew I had to do it.

Where I come from, lots of guys dream about racing
stock cars. But that was never my dream.

Dreams are for kids. And I never wanted to be a kid.
There's nothing good about being a kid.

I had faith. I knew if I kept practicing, if I got good
enough, I could be the driver.

*T*he very first time the cops caught me, I was so little they thought someone else had took the car, then ran away and left me holding the bag. They kept trying to get me to tell who had done it.

I told them the truth; it was just me. One cop slapped me. It wasn't that hard, but it hurt. I didn't cry; I was used to stuff like that.

Another cop said I was being a chump, taking the weight for the older boys. He said they would all be laughing at me while I was in jail. But they didn't even send me to jail at all, that first time.

All cops lie. All thieves lie, too, when they talk to cops. That's the way it is.

I knew that good thieves didn't lie to their partners. I wondered if cops did.

I don't remember much about the first time they locked me up, but I know it was only for a few weeks.

After that, they locked me up every time they caught me.

The first few times, it was because I didn't know how to drive. I know that sounds stupid, and I guess it was.

What I mean is, I didn't know how to drive like a regular person, so I kept bringing attention on myself. One time, I got pulled over for going through a stop sign. The cop didn't even know the car was stolen until he saw how old I was. Then he knew the car couldn't be mine.

Another time, I was just speeding, and they got me. That time, it wouldn't have mattered even if I had looked old enough to drive, because I didn't have any of the papers the cop wanted.

After a while, I figured out: If I was going to take cars, I had to drive them like I was a regular person, going somewhere.

But if I drove like that, I couldn't practice the way I needed to.

The longest they ever locked me up for was six months. Until the time I ran from the cops.

On that crazy night, I was driving past this roadhouse at the edge of town. I usually went out that way because there's a lot of places to practice. It's pretty much all two-lane blacktop with no streetlights, and even a lot of dirt roads off on the sides.

I saw a bright orange Camaro with white stripes slam on the brakes and slide on the dirt in the parking lot. I stopped the car I was driving to see what was going on; I thought maybe the Camaro was challenging someone to race, and I wanted to watch. But all the other cars around there were parked.

All of a sudden, the Camaro's door opened and a girl jumped out. She walked away, fast. The driver got out and yelled something at her, but she kept on walking. He started after her, and she turned around and ran. He chased her all the way around the side of the building.

He had left his door standing open. I could see smoke coming from the exhausts. I didn't really think about it—the next thing I knew, I was behind the wheel of the Camaro, peeling out of the parking lot.

*T*he Camaro was a terrific car, the first truly fast one I'd ever driven. I was a little disappointed that it had an automatic transmission. By then, I knew how to drive a stick real good.

I knew I wouldn't have any couple of hours that time. But it seemed like only a couple of minutes had gone by when I heard the siren and saw the flashing lights in the mirror.

That's when I made them chase me. I don't remember much about it except that I couldn't hear anything—it was like I had gone deaf or something. But it didn't scare me. Nothing scared me that night. I was driving. They were chasing me, and it felt like that was how it was supposed to be.

I was running, but I had no place to run to. And I was doing all right, until the spike strip they laid down blew out my tires.

By the time I got the Camaro stopped, it seemed like there was a dozen cop cars surrounding me. They kept coming, more and more of them. They shined big lights, so bright I couldn't look at them. They were screaming things at me, but I couldn't understand what they were saying.

I got out of the car, and put my hands up, like I'd seen people do on TV. I saw a lot of guns pointed at me. I walked toward them. They kept screaming at me.

I never saw the cop who tackled me from behind. Then

there was a lot of them. Some were yanking my arms behind my back for the handcuffs. The other ones were punching me, or kicking me, or hitting me with sticks . . . after a little while, I couldn't tell.

*T*hat time, nobody said anything about joyriding. They put a whole bunch of charges on me. The heaviest one was resisting arrest. The lawyer who came to see me in the hospital told me that.

I never had a lawyer before. Not a real one. The lawyers I had before, they were like people who worked for the court. They would be standing behind tables when I was brought out, with big stacks of paper in front of them. All they ever asked me was my name, so they could check it on their papers.

This lawyer was a little fat guy with a mustache. I told him what happened. He shook his head. Like I was stupid, and he couldn't understand what I did.

I wasn't stupid enough to try and explain it to him.

The lawyer told me I had to plead guilty to everything. If I did that, they wouldn't be too hard on me.

When I got out of the hospital, we went to court.

A couple of the cops were there. They told some lies and some truth. I did what the lawyer said. The judge asked me some questions, and I said either yes or no, depending on what he asked.

I answered the questions about how my face got all banged up and my ribs broke by saying it was from when the car crashed, even though I never hit anything.

The lawyer had told me to say it that way. When I was answering that question, I saw one of the cops looking at me. I could tell by his face that the lawyer had been right.

The judge said a lot of things about me. By the time he let the lady probation officer talk, there wasn't much point in her saying anything.

There wasn't anything good to say about me, anyway. Except that I was just a kid, and my lawyer said that a lot.

The lawyer said I had panicked when I heard the siren. That made me real mad, but I didn't say anything. He was the lawyer.

Then the judge really hauled off on me. He said I hadn't panicked at all—I was a cold-blooded felon and he didn't want to hear any excuses for my behavior. I really liked when he said that. It was like he canceled out what the fat lawyer said. I was glad I had kept quiet.

The judge said he was putting it in my record that I couldn't have a license even when I got old enough, because I was dangerous behind the wheel. I wished guys from the last place I was locked up could have been in the courtroom when he said that: "Dangerous behind the wheel."

The place they put me in after the Camaro was for the older kids. It was like a farm. We all slept in dormitories, and we had to work in the daytime.

Every dorm has a boss. A kid boss, I mean. The boss is

either the toughest or the smartest, or even both. Some-times, there's two different bosses in the same dorm—like when there's enough white guys in there to have their own gang, they would have a white boss.

There was a kid named Hector who was with us. He wasn't white, but he wasn't black either. A Mexican, is what one of the other guys said about him, but I never heard him speak Spanish. Hector said, where he was from, they called a gang a "car." So if a kid was going to join a gang, they would say he got in the car.

That sounded cool to me, except that the boss got called the driver. I didn't want to be anybody's boss, but I had to be the driver.

It was on the farm that I first met guys who did jobs. Jobs where they would need a driver, I mean. Stickup men. Those guys were in the other places I got put before, but they never mixed with amateurs like me. Joyriders. But, when I came in after the Camaro, I came in as a real thief. A thief who made the cops chase him.

Everybody wanted to know about that chase. By the time I got done telling the story, it got changed a bit. I had it lasting a hour, with them shooting at me the whole time.

I wasn't worried about anyone checking on me. I had heard that some of the kid bosses could get one of the guards to look at your records, but I knew mine was good. When I first came in, the lady who asked me a lot of questions about school and stuff also asked me about getting banged up.

"It says you received all those injuries when the car you stole crashed, Eddie. Is that true?"

The way she looked at me, I could tell she was ready to believe me if I told her different. But I said, "No, ma'am, not exactly."

She leaned toward me a little, said, "Well, what *did* happen?"

"I was okay when I got out of the car," I told her. "But then, when the cops tried to put the cuffs on me, I fought them."

"You assaulted police officers?" she said, leaning back from me, then.

"Yes, ma'am," I said.

I watched her write something on my records. I was glad. She was a nice lady, but it didn't matter what she thought of me. It didn't matter what the judge thought of me, or the cops, or anyone. Just the guys I was locked up with.

Fighting is part of doing time when you're a kid. It's not so bad, but you have to be sure to jump up when your name gets called, or they'll end up calling you "kid," in the bad way.

It's the same word, "kid," but you can always tell what it means by how people say it. Sometimes, when people say, "He's a kid," it just means he's green—he doesn't know the score. That isn't a good thing to be, but it's not such a big deal. You can always get schooled, and then you won't be green, no matter how young you are.

But if they call you some other guy's kid, that means you

do things for him. It would be better to be dead. Once in a while, that happens in there. A kid makes that choice.

There's other choices. If you're that kind of kid, I mean, if someone is trying to *make* you that kind of kid, you can go for a fence parole—that's what they call it when a kid runs.

If you try that, all kinds of bad things happen. It isn't just the beating you get when they catch you. Or even when they put you in a solitary cell and just leave you there. It's that the guys who chase you, they're the same as you.

There's a special squad of kids like that. They don't stay with us. They have their own dorm. They don't eat with us, either.

You have to be very tough to do that job, being a kid guard. Because if the *real* guards drop you down, make you go back to sleeping in the dorm with the rest of us, you're going to get hurt one night. That's a guarantee.

If the place scares you, but you're too scared to run, you can ask the bosses to lock you up in one of the solitary cells. It's safe back there. But everybody knows why you went, so you can never come out.

That's just one of the things that was so confusing when I first came in, being in solitary. If they threw you in there, like for fighting, it made you bigger. But if you went there because you wanted to, it made you smaller.

It was like driving, I thought. Just knowing the car isn't enough; you have to know the roads, too.

*E*ven if you come in with a real good charge on you, if you don't have friends Inside, you'll probably have to fight a couple of times. The charge doesn't always tell the story, so people test you.

You don't have to win when you fight, but you have to keep fighting until somebody stops it.

And if you come in without any friends, everybody watches you. They want to see what kind of a person you are. After they find out, different things happen, depending.

With me, one of the crews saw I was okay, so I got to join up. Get in the car, like Hector said. After that, the only time I had to fight was when my crew got into a beef with a different one.

*B*y the time they let me out, I knew a lot of guys who did jobs that needed a driver.

I will always remember the first one. It was one of those all-night stores that sell everything. The guy who found me, Rodney was his name, he said he used to work there, so he knew where everything was, even how to get into the safe in the back. He said they kept a lot of money in there, because they had to pay the delivery guys in cash when they came first thing in the morning, once a week.

Rodney had it all planned out, he said. A three-man job. One guy to hold the clerk, one guy to get the money, and one guy to drive.

But the night we were supposed to do it, when I went over to where Rodney was staying, him and Luther, the other guy, they were all pumped up on crystal; buzzing around like wasps in a jar, talking so fast I couldn't hardly understand a word.

They both had pistols. Rodney was waving his around, saying if the white trash motherfucker didn't hand it over, there was going to be hair all over the walls, stuff like that.

They didn't want me to steal a car. They wanted to use Rodney's. "You can pull around the back, bro," he told me. "Out where the Dumpster is. It's as dark as a toothless nigger in a coal bin back there. Nobody'll see nothing. Besides, I put other plates on it."

I wanted to tell them I wouldn't do it, but I couldn't say the words. It wasn't that I was scared. I mean, I *was* scared, but not about the robbery. I was scared, if I didn't do it, word would get around, and nobody would want me for a driver.

Rodney's car had something wrong with the mufflers. It was way too loud. You could hear the sound bounce off the sides of parked cars as we went past them.

I knew this wasn't the way to do things.

We parked off to the side, just past where the lights from the store reached.

"Let me wait here," I said. "This is better than going around back."

"Not if we have to come *out* the back, asshole," Rodney said. "Just do it like we planned."

I wanted to tell him there wasn't any plan, but it was too late for that.

"This is the slowest time," Rodney said. "Three-thirty in the morning, you never see anybody in there."

"Let's go," Luther said.

I didn't say anything. I knew who the boss was.

When Rodney told me, I pulled around the side of the store. Real slow, just letting the car creep, so the muffler noise wouldn't be so loud. They both got out. I had to hold the seatback down for Luther—a Mustang doesn't have much room in the rear.

"I'll be right over there," I told them, pointing to a big pool of shadow out past the Dumpster. Rodney was right about how dark it was.

They pulled the stockings down over their faces and looked at each other. Then they high-fived and walked away.

I turned off the lights, then I let the Mustang idle over to the spot. I backed in careful, made sure I had plenty of room. I opened the passenger door, so they could get in quicker. The little light on the ceiling went on. I popped off the cover and pulled out the bulb. Then I moved the mirror so I could see behind me.

It was hard to see good, because it was raining that night. I remember it because I was worried about the roads. I wished I'd had more time to practice driving when it was wet.

It seemed like a long time, but I guess it wasn't. I heard

gravel crunching, like people were running, then they came around the corner, fast.

They both tried to jump in the car at the same time, then Luther went in first and Rodney got in the seat next to me.

"Go!" Rodney yelled.

I pulled out slow, because I didn't know if anyone inside even knew we were back there, and I didn't want to give away what direction we went off in.

We were only a short distance away when Rodney started yelling. "Fuck fuck *fuck*!" He hit the dashboard with the butt of his pistol. "God *damn* it."

I was afraid they had killed someone, but I hadn't heard any shots.

Nobody chased us.

When we got back, I found out why Rodney was so mad. "Not even two hundred lousy fucking dollars," he said, looking at the bills spread out on the kitchen table. "They changed the deal with the safe. Dirty motherfuckers!"

Luther just kept shaking his head. He was grinning, but a lot of guys do that when they're hyped up and nervous.

Rodney divided the money three ways. I got sixty-something.

The next morning, the TV said two men had robbed the store. And got away with a little more than thirty-five hundred dollars.

I learned from that job. The more I thought about it, the better I understood what really had happened. All the time I was thinking that Rodney and Luther weren't really pros, they were thinking the same thing about me. If I was a professional driver, I never would have even gone along on that job. I would have used another car. I would have practiced with it, to make sure it was okay if the roads got slick. And I would have gotten it straight in front how much my share was.

At first, what I thought was that they didn't have a plan. Using Rodney's own car, with the bad mufflers and all, was really stupid. And getting high before they went out, that was the scariest part. I was afraid they might get so amped they would shoot someone. But it turned out they did have a plan, all along.

I didn't know about the rest of the plan for quite a while. And I only found out by accident. I was looking in the papers for an old car I could fix up, when I saw this story.

ARREST IN McMARTIN STORE ROBBERY
Two More Men Sought

The second I saw that big black type, it felt like my heart was an engine going redline. I was sure either Rodney or Luther had got themselves arrested, and whichever one it was, he had talked about the whole thing.

I'm not a great reader, but I can do it pretty good, if I go slow. Only thing, I couldn't make myself go slow that time,

and I had to read the story a couple of times before I understood it.

The guy they arrested wasn't Rodney *or* Luther. It was
the guy who worked in the store. The "inside man" is what
the police said he was. The story said it wasn't a robbery at
all. The guy who worked there, he just opened everything
up and handed it over to Rodney and Luther.

I had been a stupid kid from the beginning. Rodney's
kid, is what I felt like. It wasn't so much that they cheated
me. It was that they never needed a driver at all.

I hoped they never found Rodney or Luther. Not because
I cared about what happened to them; I was afraid they'd
tell.

Not tell the cops—I was afraid, when they went back
Inside, they would tell the other guys that I was just a stupid kid. Not a real driver at all.

Far as I know, they never caught Rodney or Luther. I figured the inside man had told on them, but the paper had
said the cops were looking for two men, not three. So probably Rodney and Luther never told the inside man they
even *had* a driver.

After that time, I was a lot more careful. I found a guy
who wanted cars stolen. He ran a big junkyard, where
he could take the cars apart and piece them out to body
shops and other places that needed different parts of certain cars.

That's what I had always told the other guys I was doing. When I was locked up, I mean. So it seemed right that

it would come true. Maybe that was part of my destiny, too.

I worked for Mr. Clanton for almost a year, doing that. He paid me depending on what the car I had to steal was worth to him, but it was never less than five hundred dollars, so I didn't have to work very often.

I got chased a couple of times, but it was different from when I was just driving with no place to go. I knew I couldn't go back to the junkyard if the cops were close on me, but Mr. Clanton told me about a whole bunch of spots where I could stash a car and just walk away . . . all I had to do was get some distance between me and the cops and bail, he said.

After a while, I got pretty good at getting into cars. I was never behind the wheel long. Mr. Clanton's place was way out of town. The last bit of road was nothing but a dirt track between the trees. I got so I could run without lights. That way, nobody could follow without me knowing.

There was a place I could pull over and wait. That was hard, sitting there with the engine off, listening for the sirens. But I had to do it. The worst thing that could happen would be for me to lead the cops back to Mr. Clanton's. He said, if I did that, they could get a search warrant, and a whole lot of people would go to jail.

When Mr. Clanton told me that, I was in his office. There was some other men there. I guessed they was the other people he was talking about.

I was driving a beautiful blue Mercedes the night I got caught. Mr. Clanton always liked them. He said a Mercedes was like a good fat pig—you could make money out of every last little piece of it.

I spotted the cop before he saw me, I think. County sheriff. Around there, the troopers worked the Interstate, the city cops had downtown, but the sheriffs' cars got to go anywhere they wanted. There's a lot of law where I come from.

It wasn't like that time with the Camaro. I wasn't speeding or anything. And I had a driver's license with my picture on it. The license was a fake. I got it from a guy Mr. Clanton sent me to. It looked real good, but I never used it, except to buy cigarettes, if I was in one of those places that asked you.

When I took a car, I always looked in the glove compartment. Sometimes people left money in there, but that wasn't what I was looking for. I wanted the registration and the insurance papers. That time I'd gotten lucky. Or, anyway, I thought I had.

So when the sheriff's car showed up behind me with its roof lights flashing, I didn't try to run.

On TV, when the cops stop someone in a car, they always call the driver "sir." The cop didn't do that with me.

I showed him the papers from the glove compartment. He told me to wait where I was, and he went back to his cruiser. I could have rabbited out of there, but I knew I couldn't outrun his radio. So I just sat there. Like that time next to the Dumpster, waiting for someone else to decide what was going to come next in my life.

The cop walked back to the Mercedes real slow. His right hand was down at his side, next to his pistol.

"Are you related to Jayne Howard?" he asked me.

"No, sir," I said. "I don't know her."

"Those papers you gave me, they say this car is owned by one Jayne Howard."

"I don't know anything about that, sir."

"Where'd you get this car, then?"

"Well, a guy came by this bar. He said he needed someone to drive his car over to Atlanta. He offered me two hundred bucks to do it."

"Is that right? Where in Atlanta?"

"The Classy Club, on Peachtree," I said. I remembered one of the guys I did time with was always talking about that place. Like it was famous or something.

The cop nodded his head like he was thinking it over. He asked me a couple more questions. I thought I was handling them pretty good, too. Until I saw the two other cruisers pull up.

The cop who arrested me told the man at the front desk that there hadn't been any trouble; I was a real gentleman. And, while they were taking my picture, I heard him tell another cop, "Ten to one, this kid never says a word. He's a real pro."

I wanted to thank him for saying that, but I couldn't figure out how to do it without sounding stupid.

After they locked me up, they asked me if I wanted to
make a phone call. I knew better than to call Mr. Clanton,
and I didn't know anyone else.

After a couple of days, they took me to court. There was
a Public Defender there. A black guy. Young. Real clean-
looking, wearing a nice suit.

He had them take me into a room where he could talk to
me private. I told him what I told the cop. He gave me a
sad smile.

Later that day, they had some kind of little trial. To
see what they were going to charge me with, I think.
Only the cop got to testify. My lawyer asked him a lot of
questions about what he did after they arrested me. It
sounded like he was saying the cop never checked out my
story.

After that was over, I went back to jail.

The lawyer came to see me again a few days later.

"You never told me you had a record," he said.

"I'm sorry."

"A record for stealing cars."

"I guess I should have," I said.

"Never mind. Just tell me the truth. That's the only way
I can help you."

"I already told you."

He showed me his sad smile again. He looked older
when he did that. "Which is it, Eddie? You think I'm dumb
enough to believe that fairy tale? Or *you're* dumb enough
to think a jury will?"

"It's all I can say," I told him.

"No, it's not. Listen. The ADA says he'll give you a sus-
pended sentence in exchange for cooperation."

I didn't know what an ADA was, but I knew what "cooperation" meant. "No," I said.

He nodded, like that was what he'd been expecting.

I t was another couple of weeks before he came back
again. He had papers in his hand, white papers, with a
blue back holding them together.

"You know what's wrong with your story?" he said. "The
ignition was popped. If it wasn't for that, for that and your
track record, I mean, you might have a fifty-fifty shot with
a jury."

"The car was running when that guy pulled up," I said.
"I never looked at the ignition."

"Uh-huh. Well, Eddie, here's the deal. Here's a deal,
anyway. You're not going to beat this case, but they don't
want to go all the way through a trial for a minor league
GTA bust. And the car wasn't banged up, so there's no
insurance company to raise hell about making an example
of you. Bottom line, they'll give you a misdemeanor plea, if
you cop."

"Cop to what?"

"Use without authority?"

"What's that?"

"Just what it sounds like," he said. "Driving the car without permission of the owner. They'll drop the Grand Theft
Auto, so no more felony. How's that?"

He looked real pleased, like he'd done extra good.

"How much time would I get?"

"First offense . . . as an adult, anyway. Misdemeanor, on a plea, we can probably seal it for six months county time."

"You mean, stay right here?"

"Yep. And with the time you've already got in, plus the time they'll take off if you stay out of trouble, maybe four months."

"I . . . don't know."

"It would be just you, Eddie," the lawyer said. "You admit to driving the car without permission, that's all. You wouldn't have to say anything else."

When I got out, I went over to Mr. Clanton's. He said I was a good, standup kid. He said he knew people who were looking for a driver like me.

That's how I ended up in the state pen. Mr. Clanton introduced me to Tim and Virgil. They were brothers. Tim was the older one, and Virgil pretty much followed his lead. I don't mean Tim was like his boss or anything; he just knew more things.

Tim was only a few years older than Virgil, but Tim always called him "kid." The way he said it, you could tell it didn't mean what it meant Inside.

The first job we did was a liquor store. I just pulled up

out front and waited while they went in. Virgil stayed by the door; Tim went all the way inside.

It seemed like only a minute when they came flying back out. I drove away fast and smooth. Never even heard a siren.

When we got to the long sweeper curve just before you could take the dirt road up to Mr. Clanton's, Tim told me to pull over. Him and Virgil got out of the car. Tim came over to my window. He said to take the getaway car to the junkyard and leave it with Mr. Clanton—only he called him Seth—and there was another car there I could use to get back.

The money was in a yellow-and-black gym bag on the front seat. Tim said to wait two days, then call him at the number I had for him. If everything was okay, I should bring him and Virgil the money then.

I wasn't exactly sure what Tim had meant by two days, so I waited until the night after the second day to call.

Tim answered the phone. He recognized my voice. Said everything was okay; told me to come over to his house.

Tim and Virgil lived in an old double-wide trailer, in a heavy patch of woods a few miles outside of town, right at the base of some little hills. They had built it out nice, with wood framing and aluminum siding. It was pretty damn big, but set so far back you couldn't see it from the road.

I knocked on the door. Virgil opened it. He moved his head to show me to come on in. Tim was sitting at the kitchen table.

"You bring the money, Eddie?" he said.

"It's right here," I told him, holding up the gym bag.

"Sit down," Tim told me. He took the gym bag from me. Held it up with one hand, like he was trying to guess the weight. "How much was in there?" he asked me.

"I don't know," I said.

"You can't count?" Virgil said.

"I never looked," I told him.

Virgil made a little noise in his throat. Tim looked at him until he was quiet. Then he unzipped the gym bag. "Let's see," he said.

He took out the money. It came in little bundles, with rubber bands around them.

"Count it," he told Virgil.

Tim lit a cigarette. He asked me if I wanted one. I said yes.

Virgil counted for a few minutes. Then he said, "One thousand, six hundred, and forty-four dollars."

Tim didn't say anything. He just stared at Virgil for a few seconds. "What did I tell you?" he finally said.

Virgil stuck out his hand for me to shake. I didn't understand why he did that, but I shook with him.

*T*im counted out some money, handed it to me. "That's six hundred," he said. "Virgil and I will split the rest. Okay?"

"Sure."

"Those package stores don't keep much cash around."

"That isn't my part," I said. "I'm the driver."

"Right. The liquor store, that was kind of like a little test run, you know what I mean?"

"I . . . I think I do. I think I do, now, anyway."

"You drive like a pro," Tim said. It made me feel a lot better than the money did.

*T*im went over to the wall, where the phone was. He dialed a number. "Your friend Rochelle doing anything tonight?" he said.

I couldn't hear what the other person said back. Then Tim said, "Oh, she'll like *this* boy, I promise you."

I don't know how much Rochelle liked me, but I liked her, all right. In the morning, I drove her to work. She was a waitress, and she had the early shift.

I saw her for a few weeks straight after that. I used some of the money from the job to buy her a bracelet she saw in a store window. Rochelle said she really liked that bracelet, so I knew I couldn't go wrong getting it for her.

One night, Rochelle told me her man would be back sometime the next day. The County was cutting him loose, and he would be moving back in with her. She said he was crazy jealous, and she couldn't be seeing me anymore.

I wasn't upset—I had never figured on a girl like Rochelle staying with me for long.

"Thank you for telling me," I said. "Otherwise, I might

have come by your house one day, and it could have been bad."

Rochelle gave me one of those looks I never understand. "Do you want your bracelet back, Eddie?" she asked me.

"It's your bracelet," I told her. "I bought it for you. I guess you could tell your man you got it from—"

"I wasn't asking you because I was worried about . . . Ah, never mind, sugar. You take care of yourself."

She gave me a kiss with no promise in it, and then she went away.

*L*ater that same night, Virgil walked over to where I was working on one of the cars in the shed.

"Rochelle was doing you a favor, Eddie," he said. "That man of hers, Leon, he is one stone insane peckerwood. You'd have to kill him."

"I guess."

Virgil was quiet for a few minutes. Then he said, "You want her bad enough to do something like that?"

"No," I told him.

"Okay, then," he said.

We smoked a cigarette apiece, just looking at the crescent moon. Then Virgil went back into the house.

*A*fter that first time, we didn't do any more test runs. Everything was for real.

One job was a post office. We went at night. Virgil was dressed in one of those padded suits people who work in meat lockers wear. Tim swung the sledgehammer against the glass. Virgil put his arms over his head and jumped right on through where it was smashed in. The alarm went off, loud.

Virgil ran around and opened the door from the inside, so Tim could help him.

The alarm kept ringing. Tim said we had to keep everything under three minutes. He told me to keep watch, but not to make any noise unless the cops showed up.

Tim and Virgil came out. They were hauling a big gray post office bag. They heaved it into the trunk and jumped in with me.

"Drive like the Devil's behind you, Eddie," Tim said.

*T*he bag was full of all kinds of stuff. Mostly stamps. There was a little cash, not much. The big score was all the blank money orders. Tim said he knew a guy who would give us a good deal on them, but we had to turn them over fast, before the feds got the list out.

One thing I learned from Tim: It was better to take a long time planning a big job than to do a lot of little ones in a hurry. After a while, I got to be in on the planning. Just the driving part, but that was very important, Tim said. Mostly the route for the getaway, but also what car to use, too.

Mr. Clanton's junkyard was so big, you could make a new car out of the parts of old ones. He showed me how to cut license plates in half and make new ones out of the pieces. Ones that wouldn't come up stolen if a cop looked at them.

"Can you get us something *really* fast?" Tim asked me one night.

"Fast top end? Or off the line?" I said. There's a big difference, but most people never think about that.

"We're *gonna* be chased, Eddie," he said. "Count on it."

"How could the cops—?"

"Not the cops," he said. "It's going to be a race. If we win, we get a *lot* of money. And nobody's going to call the cops."

"What happens if we—?"

"We get dead," Virgil said. He had a big grin on his face.

Mr. Clanton had an old Chevy stock car at his place. It used to run in Sportsman Modified over at the Speedway a few years ago. "The owner got sick of throwing away money," Mr. Clanton told us. "The fool he had for a driver spent more time on the wall than he did on the track. They never could get themselves a decent sponsor, so I took it in trade for some motors. It's just been sitting around here, ever since."

I spent a lot of time with that car. Putting in a new engine was easy—the whole front end tilted up and there was plenty of room to work. The suspension was the problem.

"This one was set up to go roundy-round," Mr. Clanton said. "Spent its whole sad life making left turns. It's geared real short, too."

I told him I was sure I could fix it, and he let me use his shop to try. Every time I made a change, I took it out and tried it, to make sure it worked.

One night, Virgil asked me what the hell was taking me so long. Before I could say anything, Tim said, "Eddie knows what he's doing."

That made me even more determined to do it perfect.

When I was done, the car looked like it was normal, if you didn't get too close. I even got the lights hooked up. There was only the one seat in the front, but we weren't going any long distance. The bad thing about it for a get-away car was that it only had two doors. If you've got more than one man coming, it takes longer to jump into that kind of car. But Tim said he had a plan for that, too.

The building was against the side of a hill, so you had to climb a long flight of outside stairs to get to the door on the second floor. That was around the side; the front was the same level as the ground—that's where they had the strip club.

"The game's upstairs," Tim said, "but the chase is going to come from around the front. They'll have to call down for help."

"What about doing their tires?" I asked him. "So they can't chase us."

"You see how many cars there are in the lot, Eddie? We don't know which ones the bouncers drive. We'd have to do them all. Anyway, there's way too much traffic in the lot, people coming in and out all the time. Anybody spots us doing the tires, we're done. You've got to *drive,* kid. All right?"

"I got it," I said. My chest felt big with what Tim had called me. Same as Virgil.

I started the engine. We rolled over to a spot right next to the bottom of the stairs. Tim and Virgil got out.

They climbed up the stairs. I lost sight of them when they went in the door.

I closed my eyes for a second, to fix the road I'd have to drive in my mind. Then I waited.

Somebody came charging down the stairs. Virgil. He grabbed the widemouth can he had stashed at the bottom, ran about halfway back up, and started splashing gas all over the steps as he backed down again.

Three shots blasted. Tim came flying down the stairs, a laundry sack in one hand. When he got to where the gas was, he threw down the sack and vaulted off. Soon as he was in the air, Virgil lit the whole thing up.

I revved the engine, put the car in first, held the clutch down.

Virgil threw the laundry sack in the side window. It landed right next to me. He crawled in behind; Tim jumped in the front. They pulled their masks off.

The flames were swallowing the stairs. I dropped the clutch. We came out of that lot like a shotgun blast. The stock car got a little sideways on the dirt, but I was ready for it to do that, and I never had to let off the gas.

The road went straight as a string for about five miles before there was any chance to turn off. I couldn't see any lights behind us.

"We're gone!" Tim said, looking over his shoulder.

We were almost to the first turnoff when I saw a pair of pickups coming toward us. Suddenly, they slammed on their brakes, blocking the road.

"Well, look at that. Hillbillies got themselves a CB radio, huh?" Virgil said. I couldn't see his face behind me, but I knew he was grinning.

I stabbed the brakes as I gunned the engine and downshifted all the way to second. As we started to skid, I cranked the wheel hard over, and floored it. The stock car got sideways, powersliding right at the two pickups. I whipped the wheel back to the left and we slipped around them with about a yard to spare.

A big chunk of the windshield disappeared just before I heard the shots.

"Come on, cocksuckers!" Virgil yelled right in my ear, blasting his pistol out the window.

Tim was somewhere under all that glass, but I could see him moving.

Everything slowed down then. I could see it all happening, like we were underwater. I felt a couple of shots go into the rear of the car, like they were going into me. Tim's face was all bloody. He was trying to get his gun up. One of the pickups wheeled around behind us. It had a row of bright lights in a bar across the top of its roof, blazing.

"Drive us, Eddie!" Tim said. Real soft, but it was like a shout to me.

I bent the stock car into that first corner, and put my right foot through the floorboard. I'd been over those roads dozens of times, practicing. It felt like there was a wire running from my hands direct into the front wheels, like I was bending my own body around those curves. Once in a while I could catch a flash of the pickup's lights on an angle, but they never got close enough to fire any more shots. At least, none I could hear.

When I spotted the big tree with the giant white "X" I had spray-painted on it, I knew we were nearly home. Just up the road a piece from the "X" was a tight hairpin curve around a mass of rocks. I could hear the pickup coming on. I braked deep, sliding just a little bit. Then I slowed down even more, so we were just barely moving. I could hear Virgil slam another clip in his pistol.

I looked over at Tim. He finally had his gun up, but he couldn't turn enough to aim back out his window.

The pickup came closer. I goosed the throttle with the clutch in, making sure the carburetor was clean. The second I saw the wash of the pickup's lights, we took off again. The stock car slipped around that hairpin like water through a pipe.

The pickup thought we were going much faster than we really were. By then, it was too late for them to slow down. I couldn't see the crash, but I heard it.

"They ain't got no more!" Virgil yelled.

When we got back, we found out that Tim was all cut up, but none of it was too bad. I didn't even know I'd been nicked until Tim's girl Merleen finished cleaning him up and came over to me.

"Your ear's bleeding, Eddie," she said.

"Probably some glass, like Tim got," I told her.

"Let me see . . . Damn! The whole lobe is about gone. You must have had a bullet go right by your face."

"I don't remember anything like that."

"It's all . . . burned, too. Like you got shot up close," Merleen said.

She poured some alcohol on my ear, then covered it with some white ointment from a tube. She wrapped a lot of tape all around my ear, real tight. It looked stupid, but it didn't hurt.

By then, I figured out what had happened, but I didn't say anything. I didn't want Virgil to feel bad.

"**Y**ou feel bad about it?" Mr. Clanton asked me.

He meant that we had to cut up the stock car and get rid of all the pieces.

"No, sir," I told him.

"That car was a *horse* for you boys," Mr. Clanton said.

I wanted to explain to him. How I didn't care about cars,

just about driving. But I thought that would sound dumb, so I just shook my head like I was sad. That was what Mr. Clanton expected of me, I think.

Virgil showed me how to bury money in mason jars, like they use for canning. Money's only paper. If you don't seal it up real tight, it could rot on you, especially if you left it a long time.

We couldn't spend most of the money right away, Tim said. The men who were in that poker game had people all over the place. If we started throwing money around, word could get back to them.

I asked Tim if he would hide my share for me.

"I'll hide half of it for you, Eddie," he said. "The other half, you have to hide for yourself."

"How come?"

"You can never have all your money in one place," he said. "What if I had to come back for my own money? In a hurry, you understand. I might not have time to cover my tracks. Anyone coming hot on my heels would find your share, too."

"If that happened, you could take my share with you."

"Eddie . . . you can't *always* get away. Not every time. If I got caught, *all* the money would be gone. Yours, too, understand?"

"I guess I do. But I could always—"

"Half," Tim said. "No more."

Virgil was a real good cook. Specially his barbeque. He made his own pit on the side of the house, out of some special bricks that came from a famous barbeque oven in Kansas City. Virgil said, after a lot of years, the bricks get to hold a flavor, and whatever you cook in them gets some of that flavor, too.

I was never sure when Virgil was having fun with me, when he told me things, but his barbeque was good enough he could have opened a restaurant. Tim was always after him to do that. He said we all had to have regular, legitimate businesses to be in, because stickup men never die of old age, and we couldn't just keep on the way we were forever.

Virgil said we were going to all do it, someday. We'd have a big barbeque joint. Virgil would be the cook, and Tim would be the manager.

"And we'll have a beautiful little garage right next to it," Tim said. "Maybe a body shop, or a place for motors. Right, Eddie?"

"Sure," I said. But I was really wishing they had asked me to work in the restaurant.

We were all out by the barbeque pit one afternoon. Virgil had been doing something with the meat all day— he had all different kinds, not just pork, like you see in some places—and he was just starting to put it on the fire. A car pulled up. An old one, is all I remember about it.

A woman got out of the front seat. She was kind of heavy, with long straight brown hair.

"Brenda," Tim said to Virgil.

The woman walked over to where we were standing.

"I got to talk to you," she said to Tim.

Tim looked over at Virgil. Then he moved his head to the side a little bit, so you could see he was listening.

"Wallace. . . ." the woman said.

"I'm not doing this again, Brenda," Tim said. "That's your man. And that's your choice. You think I forgot what happened before?"

"This is—"

"What, Brenda? This is different? How many times you come around here, looking for money because Wallace beat your ass and took your check? But that wasn't enough for you, right? You wait until I'm off somewhere and sneak yourself up here. Virgil, he takes one look at your face all bashed up, and what does he do?"

"I didn't mean for him to—"

"You're a no-good, lying bitch, Brenda," Tim said. His voice was as calm as if he was asking you if you wanted a beer. "You think, because we're kin, you get to play us over and over, don't you?"

"Tim, I swear—"

"*Don't* fucking swear," Tim said. "It wasn't the judge who sent my brother over that time, Brenda. It was you."

"I'm sorry. You know I never would—"

"You never would what?" Virgil said. His voice was soft and quiet, like Tim's. "Get me some County time for whipping that piece of shit Wallace? Yeah, you'd do that. You *did* that. But you know what, Brenda? That's not why I'm done with you, even if you are Mom's baby sister. I didn't mind doing the time. I thought it was worth it. I figured that was it for Wallace; he'd be afraid to show his mangy face around you. And then what happens?"

"Virgil. . . ."

"You take up with him again," Virgil said, still quiet. "I'm on a fucking road gang, and Wallace is back with his favorite piece of ass."

"There's nothing for you here, Brenda," Tim said. "We never thought we'd see you again, and that's the way we wanted it. You may be a stupid slut, but you're not *that* stupid, you didn't know how we felt about you. If Mom was alive, she'd spit on you for what you did to Virgil, so don't come around using her name like you did before."

"It's not for me," the woman said. Her face was all twisted up, like she was going to cry, but she didn't. "It's about Janine."

"I don't know any Janine," Tim said.

"She's Wanda and Roy's girl," Brenda said. "You know Wanda was killed by that drunk driver year before last. And then Roy took with the cancer. He's been in the hospital, just waiting to die. So I took Janine to live with me. Since I'm a blood relative and all."

"Yeah, you're a good-hearted woman, all right," Tim said. "How big a check's the government giving you for her?"

"That isn't why I did it," Brenda said. "If I didn't come through, Janine would have gone to a foster home. And you know what they're like."

"Get to it, Brenda," Virgil told her. "I got meat waiting that's more important to me than you are."

"Who's this?" Brenda said, looking at me.

"None of your business," Tim said. "*Nothing* around here is any of your business. This is a man *we* trust. You don't want to talk in front of him, tell your story walking."

"She's in the car," Brenda said.

"Who?"

"Janine. I had to bring her with me. She's only twelve. I couldn't leave her in the house alone."

"Brenda. . . ." Tim didn't sound so patient anymore.

"Wallace has been messing with her!" she said. "I just found out, I swear. I don't know what to do. She's scared of him. I can't go to the police, because—"

"You stay here," Tim said, cutting her off. "Stay here, and don't say a fucking word. Nobody's listening to you, anyway."

Tim walked down to where Brenda's car was sitting. I saw him tap on the window. In a minute or so, the window came down. I could see someone was in there, but I couldn't make out anything about them.

"I'm sorry," Brenda said to Virgil.

He acted like she wasn't there.

Tim opened the car door. A little girl got out. All I could see was that she was real skinny, with light brown hair, wearing a big yellow T-shirt that covered her all the way down to her knees. She walked down the path with Tim until I couldn't see them anymore.

They were gone a good while. Brenda kept trying to say something to Virgil, but he never spoke to her.

"Eddie, would you do me a favor?" he asked me.

"Sure."

"Go in the house and get my pistol."

"Which one?" I said.

"Any of them'll do," Virgil told me.

"Virgil. . . ." Brenda said.

By the time I got back with Virgil's pistol, Tim and the little girl were coming back up the path. Tim opened the door to the car, and the little girl got in. Tim held out his hand, and she grabbed it for a second. Then Tim came back up the rise toward us.

"Y‌ou filthy whore," Tim said to Brenda. His voice was so soft and quiet I almost couldn't hear it. "You didn't just find out about Wallace fucking that little girl. You also found out she was pregnant, huh? So now you're worried about your own ass. Like always."

"She's lying, Tim!"

"Lying about what? Lying about when she came to you and told you Wallace was grabbing her, and you slapped her face and told her Wallace was the man of the house? Lying about when Wallace whipped her with his belt until she was bloody, and you didn't do nothing? Lying about the time you woke up in the night and found Wallace in her bed?"

Tim moved closer to Brenda. She took a step back.

"Tell me, Brenda," he said. "I really want to know."

"I swear I—"

"I told you about swearing, Brenda. Remember before,

when I said if Mom was alive she'd spit on you? Well, if Mom knew what you did to that little girl, she'd fucking *kill* you, sister or no."

"What am I going to do?"

"*You,* huh? What *you're* going to do, you're going to drive Janine down to the Welfare and tell them the truth. The *truth,* you dirty bitch. If I find out you protected Wallace, I'll come looking for you, understand?"

"But if Janine tells, Wallace'll—"

"Here," Tim said, handing her some bills. "You don't go back home, understand? You go to a motel. There's enough there for a couple of weeks, food and everything. It may take a few days for the law to pick Wallace up, but he's not making bail once they do, and you'll be able to go back home."

"A motel's no place for a—"

"Janine's not going to be with you, Brenda. You leave her with the Welfare."

"But she'll end up in—"

"Wherever she ends up, it'll be better than being with you."

Brenda started crying. "You don't understand, Tim," she said. "You're not a woman."

"Neither are you," Tim said.

We were at the kitchen table later that night, when Tim said, "We've got a job, Eddie."

"Okay."

"Thing is, there's no shares this time. There won't be any money. So we'll just pay you cash, like we hired you, fair enough?"

"Sure," I said. I got up and walked outside. Quick, before anything showed on my face.

I was out there a long time. I never felt so sad in my whole life.

I heard them come up behind me. I didn't turn around.

"You want some sausage?" Virgil said. He knows it's my favorite.

"No thanks," I said.

"I don't blame him," Tim said. "Who'd want to eat a meal with a pair of stupid assholes like us?"

I didn't say anything. I knew my voice would shake if I did.

Both of them came around so they were facing me.

"We apologize, Eddie," Virgil said. "We never meant to insult you."

"It's okay," I said.

"No, it isn't," Virgil said. "We never should have offered you money. We should have just asked if you'd drive us."

I didn't want to talk. I felt like crying, only I was too sad.

"No, that's not right," Tim said. "Eddie, we shouldn't have *asked* you at all."

I looked right in his eyes.

"You're with us," Tim said. "We're with you. Blood is bullshit. Brenda's not our kin, Eddie. You are."

Right then was the best moment I ever spent on earth.

I stayed the next few days at the house. We all worked on our piece of what we had to do.

"Janine's with the Welfare," Tim said, when he got off the phone. "Nobody knows where Brenda is."

"They pick up Wallace?" Virgil asked.

"No. And they're not going to."

"How come?" I said. "Once that little girl tells who—"

"Janine's not *going* to tell," Tim said.

"Why not?"

"We made a pact," Tim said. "A blood pact, between kin. If she told, you know what would happen?"

"Wallace would go to prison?"

"Maybe. And even if he did, it'd be only for a couple of years. What's that?"

"He has to be worried, though," Virgil said. "Wondering if the hammer is going to drop."

"He's not worried about the law," Tim said. "He's worried about us."

"He doesn't know—"

"Sure, he knows, little brother. You think that whore Brenda wasn't on the phone to him first thing? Hell, she's probably with him right now. It's for damn sure Wallace hasn't been sleeping at their place. He's not going to give us a chance to catch him alone. Specially not after dark."

*T*im had a plan. We gave it a couple of weeks, then we went out to do the job.

"That's him," Tim said. "The fat fuck in the brown jacket. But there's a lot of traffic. . . ."

"It's all right," I told him, as we drove past the poolroom on the other side of the street.

The poolroom was one of those places where you could make a bet, or shoot dice, or buy different kinds of things. Out front, they had some benches, and a bunch of little tables and chairs. People played dominos and cribbage out there, or they could eat one of the sandwiches they sold inside the place. They did a lot of business.

I made another pass, then I double-backed and came at it from downwind.

Wallace was out front, at one of the tables, having a beer with a couple of other guys. It wasn't luck that we found him. Tim said he was there regular—he spent most of his days at the poolroom, either inside or out.

Virgil was in the backseat, with the window down. He had a canvas sack filled with sand draped over the sill, to make a rest for his rifle. Tim was up front, next to me. He had a pistol in each hand.

We were all dressed in the same white jackets. Tim and Virgil pulled the black stockings over their faces. We all had on black gloves. I was wearing a white cowboy hat and sunglasses.

Cars were parked in front of the poolroom, but there was space between them. I came to a stop.

Wallace never looked our way.

"Back us up just a little," Virgil said. "I need a better angle . . . yeah!"

I pulled the lever into low, held the brake down with my left foot and fed the car a little gas. I watched the left mirror to make sure we weren't going to get blocked when we pulled out. Then I said, "Okay."

A bomb went off just behind my head. Then Tim opened up with both pistols, like he was spraying with a pair of garden hoses. I moved my left foot off the brake as I stomped down on the gas.

I slipped through traffic as smooth as I could, trying to balance speed with not calling attention to us. I had to bust a red light at one corner, but that wasn't so unusual, the way people around there drove.

A few blocks later, a squad car came right at us, siren blasting. But he went on by, probably heading to the poolroom.

Once I was sure nobody was chasing us, I pulled in behind the bus depot and Virgil jumped out. He had a duffel bag over his shoulder. Inside was all three guns, the stocking masks, my cowboy hat, and two pair of gloves—I kept mine, because I was still handling the wheel.

After that, we were okay. I drove Tim all the way across town, to where he was parked. He was going to pick Virgil up from the bus depot, like he just came in from out of town.

That left me alone. I wasn't worried about an APB on the car. It was a grayish Toyota Camry; looked like a million other cars on the road. I just drove it through the alleys until I found a nice quiet spot. Then I climbed out, leaving the door open and the engine running, just like that guy in the Camaro, a long time ago.

It came out just the way Tim said it would. They had the chief of police on TV. He was a square-faced guy, wearing a regular suit. The woman asking him questions had a lot of makeup on. Her hair was blonde, stiff, like a helmet.

"The shooting appears to have been gang-related," the chief told her. "We've been charting a significant increase in drug trafficking in our area recently. We attribute this to an influx of gangs from major metropolitan areas. This is typical of their pattern; they're like salesmen trying to establish new territories."

"Is it true that you already have suspects?" the woman said.

"I don't want to comment at this time," he said. "We don't want to say anything that might compromise an ongoing investigation."

I thought maybe they were just trying to trick us, make us think they didn't know what really had happened. But then they showed the TV woman talking to a couple of the people who had been there, outside the poolroom. They both said it was black guys who had done the shooting, a whole carful of them.

We probably would have gone on forever, except for that little bank. Tim was the one who found it. He studied up on things like that, and he was a real good planner.

The bank was about an hour's drive away from where we were. It was an old one, sitting on some high ground outside the town. Tim told us the bank was there even before the town got built up, when the only thing around was the mill.

"It was a company town," Tim said.

"What's that?" I asked him.

"That's when the only work is for this one company, Eddie," he said. "Like when there's a mine, and nothing else. So the mining company owns the houses the workers live in, and it owns the stores they buy their goods in, too.

"It's like being in prison. If you have money on the books, you can get stuff from the commissary, right? Candy bars, cigarettes . . . even vitamins in some joints. And things for your cell, like a radio. But the deal is, there's only the one commissary, so you don't have a choice. If they want to sell Milky Way bars for five dollars, and you want a Milky Way bar, you pay that five dollars."

"But it's not like real prison," I said. "So how come the people in those towns, why don't they just get in their cars and drive someplace else to shop?"

"Things were different back then," Tim said. "Back when they had those company towns, if you lived there, you probably didn't have a car. Besides, you didn't have any cash money. They just paid you in scrip."

"What's scrip?"

"Like a piece of paper that you could use for money. But it was only good in the stores the company owned."

"Isn't that crooked?" I asked him.

"Our granny thought it was," Tim said. "She was the one who told me and Virgil about company towns."

"Because she lived in one?"

"Sure did. She and my granddad, a long time ago. She was a real old lady when she told us about it."

"Your granddad was a miner?"

"Not for long, he wasn't," Virgil said.

"What happened?" I asked.

"He went into business for himself," Tim said. He was smiling, like he does when he's happy.

"What business?"

"Same one we're in, Eddie," he said.

"What happened to him?"

"The law got him," Virgil said.

"He went to prison?"

"Never once," Tim said. "My granddad got shot down by the law. They came to take him, and he wouldn't go."

Tim said the bank would be swole up with money by noon every Thursday. That's because Thursday was payday at the mill, and everyone came to the bank to cash their check. The armored car made the delivery early in the morning. The first shift at the mill ended at three, so we had what Tim called a window—we had to get in and out while it was still open.

"I've been looking at that little bank for over a year now," he told me and Virgil. "There's only one guard, and he's about a hundred years old. Spends all his time jawing with the customers, like it was a general store, or something. There's only one camera, and we can take that out with spray paint. I guess there's silent alarms and stuff, but all we need is about five minutes in there, then Eddie gets us all gone."

Tim leaned way back in his chair, puffing on his cigarette like it was a big cigar.

"Boys," he said, "that little bank, it's like a cherry on top of a chocolate cupcake. All we got to do is pluck it off."

I never found out what happened inside that little bank, not until the trial.

It was just after two in the afternoon when we pulled up. Tim said that's the time it was always slow in the bank, specially on Thursdays.

Virgil had a double-barreled sawed-off. Those are good for scaring people, Tim said. Much better than a pistol. Virgil carried the shotgun under his coat, against his chest, held there by a loop of rawhide around his neck. Tim had a pair of pistols, like he always used to carry.

"Five minutes, Eddie," Tim said to me. Then him and Virgil went into the bank.

The clock on the dashboard was one of those digital ones. It said 2:09.

The clock said 2:12 when I heard the crack of a pistol. Then the boom of Virgil's shotgun.

People started screaming.

I started the engine and backed the car up to the front door of the bank.

There was more gunfire. Then it got real quiet.

I got out and opened both back doors. I jumped back in the driver's seat and watched the mirror to see when Tim and Virgil came out.

I heard the sirens, off in the distance.

I put the getaway car in gear, holding it in place with the brake.

The dashboard clock said 2:17 when the first trooper's car roared up. There was another right behind it. And then a whole bunch more.

The cops piled out. They hid behind their cars, aiming their guns at the door of the bank. One of them had a loud-speaker in his hand. He yelled at me to get out of the car and get on the ground.

I waited for Tim and Virgil.

Then the cops started shooting.

I woke up in the hospital. There were tubes running out of me. I don't know how much longer it was before I could feel the shackles around my ankles.

The cops came. And men in suits. They asked me a lot of questions. I was so dizzy that it was easy not to answer them.

The nurse had red fingernails. She was kind of chunky, but she looked pretty in her white uniform.

"Did you really rob that bank?" she asked me, real soft, when nobody was around.

"Huh?" I said.

She got a nasty look on her face. Then she picked up a big needle and gave me a shot.

One day, a lawyer came. An old guy, with a lot of heavy black hair he combed straight back. "Can you tell me what happened?" he asked me.

"Huh?" I said.

They tried us all together. All of us that was left. The lawyer showed me the papers that said they were charging Tim and me, for two counts of capital murder and four pages of other stuff. They didn't charge Virgil, because Virgil was dead.

"That second count is felony murder," the lawyer said to me. "If a person dies during the commission of a felony, everybody involved in the crime can be held responsible."

"I don't understand," I told him. It was the truth.

"The prosecution's theory is that, after the robbers had lined everyone up, one of them went into the cages. It was then that the assistant manager pulled a gun. He shot the one with the shotgun. The other robber then shot him, killing him instantly.

"The robber with the shotgun fired a blast, but it didn't hit anyone. Apparently, he was mortally wounded, and the other one wouldn't leave him. They were brothers, maybe that explains it."

I didn't say anything.

"The reason you're charged with the homicides is that you were part of the robbery attempt. The wheelman, obviously. It's not clear to me why you didn't take off before the police arrived. . . ."

He let his words trail off, the way people do when they want you to finish what they're saying. But I didn't.

I was still bandaged up by the time we started the trial, but they kept me ankle-cuffed anyway. Tim had a bunch of chains around his waist.

All the time they were putting on one witness after another, Tim never looked at me. Not once.

His lawyer never asked one single question. But when they started to bring me into it, my lawyer got up, like he had business to take care of.

"Officer," he asked the cop on the stand, "how many shots would you estimate were fired at the car in which my client was sitting?"

"I couldn't say. If he'd gotten out of the car when we—"

"More than five shots, officer?"

"I think so."

"More than ten?"

"I don't know."

"Well, officer, isn't it a fact that every single shot fired by the State Police has to be logged in and accounted for? Every single bullet?"

"Yes, sir."

"Can you tell us where we would find out that information, please? Where is it all collected?"

"That would be with the shooting team," the cop said. He was watching my lawyer like a bird on the ground watches a cat.

"That team reviews all police shootings, to determine if they were justified, is that correct?" my lawyer asked him.

"Yes, sir. And this one was perfectly—"

"I'm sure," my lawyer said. "Now if I were to tell you that the report of the shooting team was that seven different officers fired a total of thirty-one rounds at the car in which my client was sitting, would that surprise you?"

"No."

"Thank you. Now, after my client was wounded and taken into custody, you examined the interior of the car, did you not?"

"Yes."

"How many guns did you find in the car, officer?"

"There were no weapons in the car."

"By 'weapons,' do you mean firearms, officer? Or are you referring to weapons of any kind, such as a knife or a club?"

"Weapons of any kind."

"I see. And did you search the trunk of the car as well?"

"Yes."

"With the same result?"

"No weapons were found in the trunk of the vehicle," the cop said. His jaw was clenched so tight you could see a knot in his cheek.

"Were any weapons found on the person of the defendant?" my lawyer asked him.

"On . . . ?"

"On *my* client, officer. The young man sitting right over

there, at the counsel table. You see him, the one with all the bandages?"

"No."

"No, you don't see my client? Or, no, you didn't find any weapons on my client after you shot him?"

"Your *honor*!" the DA said.

The judge stared hard at my lawyer, but anyone could see he didn't scare him any.

There was a lot of stuff like that, but I didn't see what the point of it was. I saw a couple of people on the jury looking at me, but I couldn't tell what they were thinking.

When they called Tim's name, it was like a shock wave hit the place. I guess nobody expected him to get on the witness stand and talk for himself. I know my lawyer told me he wouldn't let *me* do it.

But Tim didn't act like himself up there. Tim was a man with a lot of charm. That's what Merleen, Tim's girl, told me once. I wasn't sure exactly what it meant, although I knew it was true.

On the stand that day, you would never know Tim had any charm at all. It was like he was sneering at everyone. Like they were all nothing but bugs.

He said him and Virgil were professional robbers. They'd robbed dozens of places and nobody ever got hurt. "And if that punk manager hadn't tried to be a hero, nobody would have gotten hurt this time, either," Tim said. "The little asskisser was trying to show what a good boy he was, save the boss's money. He shot my brother in the back, like the weasel coward he was. I wish I could kill him again."

A woman started crying, real loud. I guessed maybe she was the wife of the man Tim had shot. The judge had to bang his hammer hard a few times to get people to quiet down.

Tim told them that, after Virgil got shot, he wasn't able to move, and Tim couldn't carry him and keep his gun on everyone at the same time, so he just dug in and waited for the cops, so they could get Virgil an ambulance.

"My brother was still alive when they took him out of there," Tim said. "I figure the cops took their time getting him to the hospital."

His lawyer tried to clean that one up. "You're not saying the police are responsible for your co-defendant's death?" he said.

"Between them and that little weasel in the bank, they got it done," Tim said.

"Look at his eyes!" someone whispered behind me. "He's a psycho."

The judge slammed his hammer again, until people stopped making noise.

Tim and his lawyer were staring at each other like a pair of pit bulls on the scratch line. Finally, the lawyer shrugged his shoulders, like there was nothing he could do about things. He stepped back, away from Tim, and said, "You know a man was arrested outside the bank, don't you?"

"You mean Eddie?" Tim answered him. "Yeah, I knew that."

"Was he your accomplice?"

"Accomplice? *Eddie?* Be serious. Virgil and I always do things the same way. We plan out a job, then we find some dummy to drive us. They usually never know what's going on, unless someone starts chasing us.

"Eddie, he's not real swift in the head. All we told him was, if he'd drive us to the bank, wait for us, and then drive us back home, we'd pay him a couple hundred bucks. Hell, we didn't even tell him the car was stolen."

"He went too far with that one," my lawyer whispered. "Now he's opened the door."

W hen it was the DA's turn at Tim, he practically jumped out of his chair.

"Are you claiming your acts were justified?" he yelled.

"Which acts?" Tim said, grinning at him.

"Murder!"

Tim lifted his shackled wrists so he could point his finger at the DA. "That wasn't murder," he said. "That was justice." Tim's voice was like stone. "That coward killed my brother, and I killed him."

The DA stuck his chest out, talking real loud. "If you and your brother hadn't robbed that bank, this never would have—"

"Me and Virgil robbed *plenty* of places," Tim cut him off. "And all that time, we never shot nobody. Never beat anyone up. Never raped any of the women. If that punk had just kept his hand in his pocket, he'd still be alive. And me and Virgil would be down on the beach in Biloxi, spending that bank's money."

"You and Virgil and your co-defendant, you mean?"

"What co-defendant? You mean Eddie?"

"That's right. Your poor, innocent friend Eddie. You testified earlier that he didn't even know the car he was found in had been stolen, is that correct?"

"That's right."

"Would it surprise you to know that your friend Eddie has been to jail for stealing cars?" the DA said. He stepped off a little, like he had just landed a good one.

"Hell, no," Tim laughed at him. "Eddie's a natural-born sucker. Fifty to one, somebody else stole those cars, and left Eddie to take the weight.

"That boy's not all there in his head. He couldn't plan to take a shower. Look at what he did, for Christ's sake. We tell him to wait for us, and so he just sits there. And when the cops start blasting, he *still* sits there, like a lump of clay."

I could feel people looking at me. I didn't want to look at them, and I didn't want to look down, like I was afraid. For the first time, I looked at Tim.

"Eddie's not like other guys," he told the jury. "He's a retard. Slow." Tim's eyes were like chips of blue ice.

"It's like Eddie's just a kid," he said, shaking his head. "A simple, dumb kid."

The jury found me guilty of something, some charge I never heard of. I wasn't guilty of the killing, or even of the robbery. I guess it probably had something to do with the car I was in.

My lawyer was really happy. He said the most the judge could give me would be five years, and I probably wouldn't get even that much.

"I guess you heard how Tim made out," he said.

I just shook my head.

"Capital murder," the lawyer said. "And the jury found special circumstances. Do you know what that means?"

I shook my head again.

"It means the death penalty," the lawyer said. "If he hadn't come across like such an outlaw when he testified, they might have cut him some slack, I think. It wasn't an intentional murder. I would have thought a life sentence would be more appropriate, myself."

"Yeah," I said.

The lawyer looked at me hard, like he could stare through to the truth. I think he was mad because he knew I would never trust him.

When you first come into prison, they keep you separate from everyone for a few weeks. They have to make sure you don't have a disease, I guess. Once in a while, they bring you out of your cell to see a doctor or to talk to different people. Everybody asks you a lot of questions.

One man, I guess he wasn't a guard, because he didn't have a uniform, it was his job to tell new guys what prison is like. I know that because he started to tell me stuff like don't borrow money from anyone. He was reading through a bunch of papers while he was talking to me, moving his finger down the pages.

"Oh, you've been in the system for a long time," he said.

"I guess," I told him.

"Well, then you already know the score," he said.

It was in prison that I first learned what I was. I mean, what to call myself: a getaway man.

I learned that from J.C. He was an older guy, maybe forty or something. He was a heist man. You don't get called that if you just stuck up a bunch of 7-Elevens, or even if you broke into places. You had to be doing big jobs, like banks. The way Tim wanted.

J.C. had so much respect in there that the blacks left him alone, even though he wasn't with any of the gangs. That's really hard, to do time by yourself, no matter how much you might want to. Even the guards treated him good.

I never thought a man like him would ever talk to me.

One day, a guard came around to my cell. He told me I was being discharged into population. I went with him into the main part of the prison.

They gave me a cell. I could see right away it wasn't a good one. Too close to where they have to rack the bars to let you off the block, so it would be noisy all the time. But at least I was the only one in it.

The first thing I did when I got to go out into the yard

was to look around for guys I'd been with in the kiddie camps. We all knew we'd go to prison someday, and some of us made promises, to stick together and everything, when we met up again. But I didn't see any of the guys I knew from before.

Except for one—Toby. When I first spotted him, he was walking with the boss of one of the white power gangs. I watched until he went off by himself. I figured Toby could talk me up with the gang; get me in, too.

But when I came up to him on the yard, Toby wouldn't talk to me. He acted like he didn't know me at all. His eyes had colored stuff on the lids, like a girl's. And when he walked away, I could see someone had cut the back pockets off his jeans.

Where we were before, Toby had never been anybody's kid. I could see the state prison was different. That made me nervous, but I knew I could never show that to anyone.

That was the same day I met J.C. I was standing by myself, watching Toby walk away, wondering what I was going to do. I didn't know that much about prison, but I knew I couldn't make it in there all by myself.

J.C. just walked up to me, and asked me how I got there.

You're not supposed to do that, I know. Not when you're in a real prison, for grownups. But J.C. was bigger than the rules. I had to answer him. His voice was like the stuff they put in air conditioners. That stuff is so cold you can't touch it or you'll get burned. J.C. had a couple of guys with him. Older guys. Their eyes didn't have anything in them at all.

"I was the driver," I told him.

"Yeah, I know that," J.C. said. I wondered how he could know, but I didn't say anything.

I guess a couple of minutes went by before J.C. realized I wasn't going to say anything else, not unless he asked me to.

"How come you didn't get in the wind when you first heard the shots inside the bank?" he asked me.

"Tim and Virgil were still there," I said.

"You heard the sirens, right? You knew the cops were rolling?"

"They were still inside," I told him.

He looked at one of the guys with him. I'd seen that look before.

"That was solid," J.C. said. "That's the first thing a real getaway man has to have. Balls. No nerves, and balls of steel. Am I right?"

One of the other guys said he was. I didn't think he was asking me.

A few nights later, I went off the block. I knew I couldn't just stay in my cell all the time, or people would get ideas about me.

I didn't know when the test would come, but I wanted it to be where there would be guards close by.

I went over to the rec room, to watch the TV. There were plenty of empty chairs.

In just a minute, a black guy came over and sat down next to me. He was my height, but much wider. He had huge muscles all over him, like armor. He was smiling, friendly. His teeth were very white. I didn't look in his eyes. He smelled clean and bitter, like laundry soap.

This was the test. I knew what would come next. If I talked to him, he'd see if my voice was under control. If I sounded scared, then he'd be nice. Tell me what a bad place the prison was if you didn't have a friend. Maybe offer to protect me from certain people in there, pat my arm to make me feel better. Then he'd ask me to go someplace with him. Someplace where we could talk.

But if I didn't answer him, he'd pretend to get mad. He'd say I had disrespected him, or something like that.

It didn't matter how he was going to get it started, it was always going to end the same way.

I knew I'd have to try and hurt him bad, if I ever wanted to be left alone. My best bet was to jump him first, but I was, like, paralyzed, trying to make myself move.

There was only one guard in the rec room. He was watching the TV.

I was looking at the floor, trying to see if there was anything I could use on the black guy. I wished I had a knife. I didn't know how to use one—I mean, sure I knew how to use one, but I'm not a pro at it, like some guys you hear about when you're locked up—but I know, some people, if you just show them a blade, they'll back off.

I didn't think that black guy would back off, even if I had a knife. I could tell he'd done this before.

I wished Toby hadn't done what he did.

The black guy was talking to me. I couldn't make out any words—just the sound, like my ears were full of water.

I knew it had to happen soon.

And then another black guy came up to us. He was older

than the one who was trying to bulldog me; he even had gray in his hair.

I snuck a peek around the room, but everybody was looking away from us.

The older guy didn't say anything. He just shook his head at the one sitting next to me—side to side, like he was saying no.

The guy with all the muscles got up, like he just remembered something he forgot to do.

The two black guys walked off together. Nobody else came over. I sat by myself for the whole rest of TV time.

A couple of days later, J.C. and his men found me again. They stood around me, but I didn't feel all hemmed in; I felt safe.

"At the trial, Tim took all the weight, didn't he?" J.C. said. "Told the jury you didn't even know what was going on. Just a dumb kid he and his brother talked into driving them to the bank. That's why you're only doing a nickel, not sitting up in the death house with Tim."

"I never said anything," I told him.

"At the trial? Why should you? Tim was putting it all on him and his brother. And his brother, he didn't make it. All you had to do was sit there."

"I didn't say anything even before that. When the cops had me."

"Why not? They must have wanted you to roll over, testify against the others. Offered you a deal."

"I would never do that," I said.

He looked at the guys with him again. But it was a different look, that time.

*A*fter that, I was with J.C. Everybody knew it.

J.C. was short—near the end of his sentence—when I met him. He got out almost two years before me. But, by that time, it was okay—I could live there by myself. It was like J.C. had left his protection on me.

One night, before he left, J.C. told me I didn't want a parole.

I nodded okay.

"That doesn't sound crazy to you, Eddie? What I just said?"

"Not if you say it," I told him.

Then J.C. explained: If I was going to be a getaway man, I couldn't have some parole officer checking on me all the time. A good getaway man is responsible for everyone who goes out on the job. He has to get them home safe.

"What if your P.O. just dropped in the same day you were working?" J.C. said. "You're not home, that isn't going to stop him. Those motherfuckers don't need a warrant to search your house if you're on parole. You see what that could do?"

"Yeah," I said.

"For you, parole is a chump play," J.C. said. "With good time and all, you'll max out only a few months later, anyway. If you were doing thirty years, and they offered you a parole after ten, well, you'd *have* to take that. But with the time you've got, it doesn't make any sense to expose your-self."

The parole board was easier than I thought. J.C. had told me a few tricks I could use to mess things up, but I didn't need any of them.

The parole people asked me if I felt any remorse for the man who was killed inside the bank. I knew they didn't mean Virgil. I told them I had nothing to do with what happened, like J.C. told me to. One lady on the board said I had to learn to take responsibility. She said that a lot. I told her I didn't do anything.

They all started yelling at me, then. I didn't answer them back. And I didn't get the parole.

When I'd paid everything they said I owed, they let me out. J.C. was right—it wasn't much longer than if I'd gotten that parole.

Prison's full of guys who have gotten out before, and come back. They always complain that your clothes get old while you're locked up. So when you make it out, the first thing you need to do is get some clothes that are in style.

I guess the good thing about the kind of clothes I wear is that they don't get old. I was glad of that, because I only had the fifty dollars gate money they give you, plus sixteen dollars on the books from my job on the cleaning crew in Four Block.

They pay your bus fare back to your hometown. If you don't have a hometown, you can go anyplace in the state you want, one-way.

I took the bus west, just like J.C. said. At the end of the line, I walked over to the highway and thumbed a ride. It didn't matter to me where the guy was going, but I remembered not to say that. All I really needed was to get to another town, so I could get on another bus, and go back east, away from the flatlands.

I did everything in order. First, I got a room. J.C. told me how to find the place. It was in a part of town where everybody writes on the walls. A four-story house, all busted up into tiny little rooms, not much bigger than my cell.

The walls were gray, and the shade over the window was the yellow things get from cigarettes after a long time. The shade was taped in a lot of places. The bed had a big drop in the middle. The sheet was the same color as the walls. There was a wire strung across the room on one side, so you could hang your clothes. A little lightbulb swung down from the ceiling—you had to reach up to turn it on or off.

I couldn't see a place in the wall to plug in a radio, if I had a radio. The toilet was down the hall. Some of the people who used it must have been drunk.

I asked the man downstairs if there was a phone. He said no. I just walked around until I found one, outside a store. I called the number J.C. gave me. It rang three times, then a girl's voice came on.

"Hi. We're out having fun. If you know how we can have some more, leave us a message. Bye!"

I wasn't surprised by this. J.C. had told me it would be a machine.

"This is Eddie," I said. "I just got—"

"Are you staying where you're supposed to be?" a voice cut in. A man's voice, but not J.C.'s.

"Yes. I went right to—"

"Stay there," the voice said. Then it hung up.

That was almost four years ago. I'm a getaway man now. Seven jobs, every one correct. We never got caught. Only got really chased once. And that was by a city cop's car—it didn't have a chance. All I had to do was to put a couple of corners between us, and we were gone.

We don't stay together, except just before a job and for a little while after. The cops always expect us to run far, but we never do. That's what I mean about a couple of corners. We have other cars—switch cars, they're called—stashed.

Whatever car I drive, we drop that one off quick, and jump into one of the switch cars. And even then, we only go a little ways. There's plenty of places to stash cars in this part of the state, now that the plants have all pretty much closed down. Lots of empty buildings, all the windows broke out.

Nobody on the job ever goes right back to where he lives, either. J.C. rents places where we all stay for a while. That way, no neighbor sees you leave just before a job, or come back right after one. Those are the kinds of things cops look for.

Everybody wears gloves, so we can just walk away from the getaway car when we switch. But they can find out stuff from blood, too. One time, J.C. got hit. It wasn't bad, but he was bleeding a lot. So, that time, we couldn't just dump the getaway car. I dropped J.C. and the other guys off; they took the switch car, and I went back out.

I drove the getaway car until I got it way back on a dirt road I knew about. I siphoned a five-gallon can of gas out of the tank, and I poured it all over the backseat, where J.C. had been bleeding. Then I wadded up a rag into an empty soda bottle and poured a few drops of the gas over the top. I lit the rag. As soon as it got going a little bit, I tossed the bottle underhand through the back window. Flames shot right up, and I knew there wouldn't be a trace of J.C.'s blood left.

I walked back through the woods to a main road, where I knew there would be phones. I figured it would take a few hours, and it would be dark by then.

I'd only gone a little distance when I heard a big air-sucking noise. I looked back, but the woods were thick, and I couldn't see anything.

*A*ll the jobs I did with J.C., I was always the driver. But I wasn't a getaway man all the time. Sometimes, I would take the bus to a big city up north. When I got there, I would go to wherever J.C. said. I could never take a cab to those places; J.C. says that cabdrivers have to keep records, and we never wanted to be on anybody's records.

"The perfect driver would be an invisible man," J.C. told me. "Driving an invisible car."

When I would get to the places I was supposed to, I would ask for a particular person. Most of the time, it was a man, but once it was a woman. They would give me a car to drive.

That was all I had to do, then. Drive the car. A long distance, it always was. When I got to where the car was supposed to be, I would just drop it off. The people I dropped it off with would make me wait while they checked to see if everything was all right. It was always all right.

Then they would take me to a bus station, and I would go back to wherever I was living.

I asked J.C. once, if I got stopped by the police, should I try to get away from them.

"No, Eddie," he said. "Remember, you were hired to transport a car from one place to another, that's all. You're getting paid by the mile. Lots of guys do that kind of work. If you ever get busted, you make sure they give you a polygraph."

"A lie detector?"

"Right. Because the only question they're going to care about is whether you knew what was in the trunk. And you're going to pass, understand?"

J.C. knows how to plan things out. He told me, on those drives, I should always carry a decent amount of cash, but never a gun.

All the times I drove those cars, there was always a spare tire—one of those little ones that will take you far enough to buy a new tire—and a jack, on the floor of the backseat. Never once did I ever have to open the trunk.

None of these people paid me. They paid J.C., and he would give me my share whenever I got back.

*S*ometimes, I had to lay over a day or two after I dropped a car off, in case they had another one for me to take out.

One time, the place where I was staying was near a mall. A huge one, with a lot of real classy stores in it. Usually, whenever I had time on my hands, I would go to the movies. But that day, I remembered something I had been wanting to do, so I walked over to the mall.

I wanted to get something for Bonnie. She wasn't my girlfriend, exactly—I had just met her a few weeks before—but I had hopes.

I'd met Bonnie in Wal-Mart. I went to get a pair of boots, and she worked there. Not over where you get shoes, but where they had jackets and stuff.

Bonnie had red hair and real white skin. She had freckles, too, like cinnamon dusted over milk.

"You could use a new coat to go with those new boots," she said, as I was walking by with the box the boots had come in.

She had a beautiful smile. It was so wide, it made her eyes kind of scrunch up.

"This one's still pretty good," I told her.

"Good for what?" she said. "It's kind of tired. I'll bet your girlfriend has been after you to get rid of it."

"No."

"No, she hasn't. Or, no, you don't. . . ."

"I don't have a girlfriend," I told her.

"Good!" Bonnie said. She was kind of bold, but she was so nice about it that you'd never think she was slutty.

I didn't really know how to ask a girl for a date. Most of the girls I ever knew, I just met them in places I was. Like when they'd come over to Tim and Virgil's. Or in a bar. But I never liked to talk to girls in bars—it seemed, half the time, that ends up with you getting in a fight.

The girls who came over to Tim and Virgil's always talked good about men who took them to nice places. I wasn't sure what that meant, exactly, but I knew they didn't mean the movies. I stood there like a damn stump, trying to remember what it was they said they liked. And, then, I remembered. So I asked Bonnie if she would like to have dinner with me.

I could see in her eyes that it was the right thing to say. She gave me her address, and told me to come around eight. It was a Friday, but she didn't have to work late, she said, because she started at seven in the morning.

Eight o'clock seemed pretty late to be eating dinner to me, specially if you got started so early in the day, but I didn't say anything.

*A*ll that afternoon, I tried to puzzle it out. I didn't know what Bonnie meant by "around eight," for starters, but I figured I'd come there at eight exactly, so I could handle that one. It was the going out to dinner part that confused me. I had asked her easy enough, but I didn't have a plan, so I was a little nervous.

One thing I knew—I couldn't take her to Denny's or McDonald's or anyplace like that. I looked in the paper.

There were so many places I couldn't believe it. I didn't know how to choose.

So I just started calling them. But when I would ask how much a meal cost—I figured that was a good way to tell if it was a classy place—they treated me like I was stupid, and I got all embarrassed.

Finally, I just went out looking for myself. I drove past a lot of restaurants until I saw one that looked pretty nice. I parked and walked up to it. And, sure enough, there was a menu right in the window.

It was *real* expensive, that place, so I knew it had to be a good one. Enrico's, the name was.

I got back to where I was staying, and I took a shower and shaved extra careful. When I went to get dressed, I was all embarrassed again—I could see what Bonnie meant by me needing to get a new coat.

I had money. Ever since I got out of prison and started working, I always had money. J.C. and the others spent their money on all kinds of things, but I never spent most of mine. When they would ask me if I wanted to go to one of the gambling clubs, I never much did.

J.C. knew how to dress. His clothes didn't look real fancy, but, somehow, you knew they cost a lot of money.

Tim and Virgil spent money on clothes, too, but you never had to look close to see that. One time, we were all supposed to go over to this roadhouse where a band Tim liked was playing. Virgil said there would be a lot of girls there, and I couldn't go looking like I was. He went and got one of his shirts—a beautiful red silky one, with gold stitching and pearl buttons—and he told me I had to wear it. I was worried about getting it torn—I had been to that same roadhouse with them before—but Virgil said there was no point in having nice clothes if they were going to stay in the closet.

I didn't give Virgil his shirt back right away. I wanted to get it all cleaned and ironed first. But when I brought it over to him, he told me I needed to keep it, because it didn't fit him anymore. Besides, he said, he knew the shirt had brought me luck.

That made me embarrassed, but it felt good, too.

I never knew what happened to that shirt. I wasn't wearing it when I got shot and arrested and all, and there was no one I could ask to go over to where I was staying and get my stuff. Maybe the cops got it.

But J.C. didn't live near me, the way Tim and Virgil had, so I couldn't go over and ask for advice. J.C. wasn't the kind of man you could just show up at wherever he was staying, anyway, even if you knew where that was.

I went out to the stores. It took me quite a little while, but I found a real nice shirt. Not a red one, a dark blue one.

*B*onnie lived with her mother. She introduced me, and her mother asked me what I did for a living. I told her I was a mechanic—J.C. said to never tell people I was a driver; they wouldn't understand it.

Bonnie's mother asked me where I worked, and I said I worked for myself.

"You're pretty young to have your own shop," she said.

"Well, it's not really a shop, ma'am," I said. "It's just a garage behind the house I rent, but it's got a lift, and industrial wiring for my tools."

"You work off the books, then?"

"Mama!" Bonnie said. "That's not your business."

"No, ma'am," I said. "I got a bank account for my business. And I pay my taxes regular, too." I felt proud saying that. And I was thinking how smart J.C. was. It was him who told me I had to have a legitimate business.

"It doesn't matter if you *make* any money, Eddie. Just so you *deposit* some money. In the bank. You have to account for the money you spend, so the government doesn't get suspicious. We all have little businesses," he said. "Cash businesses. Like a parking lot or a cigarette store. You see what I'm telling you?"

"I . . . think so."

"You have to pay taxes," J.C. said. "You don't pay taxes, they know you're doing crime. A smart thief always has a good civilian front."

"Hah!" Bonnie said. "Not the answer you expected, huh, Mom?"

Bonnie's mother laughed. "Fair enough," she said. "I apologize, young man. But Bonnie's my only child, and you know how that is, don't you?"

"Yes, ma'am," I said.

It was almost nine when we got to Enrico's, the restaurant I had picked out. When we got inside, there was a man standing behind a little desk.

"May I help you?" he said to me. He didn't sound like he wanted to help me.

"We want to eat dinner," I told him.

"You, uh, have reservations, I trust?"

"I didn't . . . I mean, I thought we could. . . ."

Bonnie grabbed my arm and pulled a little, so I had to lean down toward her.

"I don't want to eat here, Eddie," she said. "I heard bad things about this place. About the food, I mean. Can't we go somewhere else?"

"Sure," I said. "But I don't know any—"

"Oh, I know a *wonderful* place. Do you like Chinese food?"

The restaurant we went to was just like I would have picked out, if I had known what I was doing. We had a whole big booth to ourselves. There was all kinds of different food, and I liked every bit of it.

I was really glad that Bonnie had known Enrico's had such a bad reputation. The Golden Dragon was a million times better, even though it didn't cost anywhere near as much.

After that, we went out three more times. To the Golden Dragon twice, and to a club, once. But Bonnie didn't favor the club. I was glad—I don't like it when it's very loud, either, but I thought she might have gotten tired of just going out to eat.

She always looked so pretty. Not just when we were

going out, but all the time. Once, she came by my garage on a Sunday, just to have a soda with me. She was wearing a pair of overalls and a white T-shirt with short sleeves. I remember how her arms looked in that shirt, all nice and round.

I hadn't said anything to Bonnie about going away for a few days. I didn't want to act like it was a big deal; I mean, that it would be a big deal to her if I was going to be out of town for a while.

I planned on asking her to the movies when I got back. And I thought, if I got her a nice present, she would know that I hadn't forgot about her just because I was away. I thought her mother would like that, too. Not a present for herself, but that I got Bonnie one. Her mother was that kind of person, I could tell.

I was thinking about maybe a little bottle of real good perfume. The girls I knew from Tim and Virgil were always saying how much they loved perfume. Clothes and jewelry and perfume. It would make me too embarrassed to be buying girl's clothes, and I didn't know anything about jewelry—Rochelle had picked out that bracelet her ownself. So I figured on the perfume.

In the mall, I couldn't find a place with bottles of perfume in the window. But I did find one with store dummies all dressed in clothes you knew had to cost a lot of money, so I went in there.

The place was really big. Not as big as a Wal-Mart or a Sam's Club, maybe, but it was three stories, and it sold all different kinds of stuff.

I wasn't sure where to go, so I just walked around. I was feeling good inside. I had money in my pocket and I was dressed all neat. Nobody knew me in that city. If anyone saw me, they would think I was a regular man. Maybe one who had a job in a place where I made a good salary. A man who had a wife and kids, and a nice little house.

That's when I first saw Daphne. And if I'd been a regular man, I would never have known what she was doing.

She was a tall girl, kind of skinny, with short yellow-blonde hair. She was wearing a shiny black dress and high heels. She looked very classy, like one of those window dummies come to life.

When I first saw her, she had her pocketbook—a black, shiny one, just like her dress and her shoes—open at the top. It was on a strap over her shoulder, dangling down by her waist. She picked up a wristwatch from one of the counter displays with her left hand. Then, quick as a flash, she cut something off it with a little pair of scissors in her right hand, and dropped the watch into her pocketbook.

She moved away from the counter, just taking her time and looking around, like she couldn't decide what to buy.

By the time she was close to the escalator, she had put a few more things in her bag. A lipstick, I saw for sure. And a little white jar of something.

That's when I saw the man watching her. He had on a dark green sport coat, and a white shirt with no tie. He went everywhere the girl did, but never all that close. A young guy, kind of pudgy, with a bully's look on his face.

At first I thought he was working up his nerve to talk to her. But then he turned to look over his shoulder, and I saw the walkie-talkie clipped to his belt.

I knew there wasn't much time. And I knew I was being stupid, but I still went over to the shelves where the girl was looking at those little tiny computers you can put in your pocket.

"Excuse me, ma'am," I said.

She looked up real quick. There were two dots of red on her face, one on each cheek. Her eyes were very big. Her mouth was open a little bit.

"There's a man been watching you. He's been watching you put stuff in your purse. I think he works for the store."

She turned her back on me and walked away, moving smart, like she was about business. She marched right over to one of the registers, and started taking stuff out of her pocketbook. A woman came over from behind the counter. I couldn't hear what they said to each other but, finally, the woman behind the counter rang up all the stuff the girl had. The girl took out a credit card.

The pudgy guy in the suit coat walked past me. He gave me one of those "I'll know you next time" looks, but he didn't say anything.

I finally found where they sold the perfume. A nice older lady with a pearl necklace sold me a tiny little bottle for more than fifty bucks, so I knew it was really good stuff.

She asked me if it was for Valentine's Day. I could tell by the look on her face I should say yes, so I did.

"Then you'll want it wrapped," she said.

She put it in a little box that was just the right size. Then she wrapped it in shiny silver paper, and put a thin red ribbon all around it, tied in a bow.

*B*y the time I left, it was the middle of the afternoon. I was a little hungry, so I thought I'd look for a place where they sold food. I never knew a mall that didn't have them.

"Hey," a woman's voice said.

I turned around. It was the girl from the store, the one in the black dress.

"That was very chivalrous of you," she said.

I didn't know what she meant, but I could tell from the way she said it that it was something good.

"That's all right," I said.

"I've been waiting for you. The least I could do is buy my rescuer a drink."

She took hold of my arm and steered me down the corridor. I thought we were going to a bar, but she kept going until we were in the parking lot.

"Where's your car?" she said.

"It's in the shop," I told her. Which was kind of the truth.

"How did you get here, cab?"

"That's right," I said. Which wasn't true, but I didn't want her to know I was staying so close by. Or the kind of place I was staying in, either.

"Then we'll take mine," she said, and started steering my arm again.

After we walked a little bit, she reached in that pocketbook of hers and took out some keys. She had one of those things that unlocks your car from a distance. When she pressed on it, I heard a chirping sound. I looked in that direction. There was a big Lexus sedan, plum-colored, with its lights blinking.

"That's mine," she said. "Do you like it?"

"I never drove one," I told her.

"Then you should drive this one," she said, and handed me the keys.

I wanted to explain to her that I didn't mean I wanted to drive that car; I just couldn't say if I liked a car if I'd never driven that kind. But I didn't say anything.

"You drive very . . . carefully," she said, after we'd gone a few blocks.

"I'm getting the feel of it," I told her. "You have to do that a little bit at a time."

"Oh. Are you a professional driver?"

I liked the way that sounded in her mouth. "That's right," I said. "Driving is what I do."

"Do you race cars?"

I liked her for saying that. I was afraid she was going to think I drove a cab, or something like that.

"No, not that kind of driving," I said.

"Well, do you like the car *now*?" she asked me.

"I still don't know yet. You really can't tell about a car unless you put it through its paces."

"Like a horse?"

"I . . . guess so. I don't know anything about horses."

"Like a test drive," she said. "Only a hard one, yes?"

"Yeah. That's it."

"All right," she said. "I know where you can do that. Turn left at the next light."

We ended up on a farm. Not a farm where people grow things, just a place with a lot of land. I know it belonged to someone rich, because there was a gate to get in. She pushed a button on a box she had clamped to the sun visor, like one of those garage door lifters, and the gate opened right up.

"Is this yours?" I asked her.

"My father's."

"It's a big place."

"Not so big," she said. "If you know what I mean."

I didn't know what she meant, so I just nodded. That satisfies most people.

"Is this a good spot?" she said, after a little while.

It was a single strip of blacktop, laid down like a runway for an airplane. Grass on one side of it, dirt on the other.

"Does it curve at all?"

"Up ahead it does."

"Okay," I said, and stomped the gas.

The car was faster than I would have thought, big as it was. Got around turns pretty decent, too, although it heeled over a bit. At the end of the stretch, I slammed on the brakes. The car didn't skid at all, just scrubbed off speed in a straight line. Just as I got it stopped, I flipped the lever into reverse and floored the pedal. We went flying backwards. I spun the wheel all the way to the right and slammed it down into drive as I gave it the gun and cranked over to the left. We went steaming on back the way we came.

"Wow!" she said. "What was that?"

"It's called a bootlegger's turn," I said. "In case you have to reverse yourself real quick."

"Do it again!"

I thought she wanted to see how I did it, so she could do it herself, but no matter how many times I showed her, she never asked to try.

It worked even better on the dirt road.

"Pull over there," she said, after a while. "I never smoke in the car."

I could tell *somebody* smoked in that car, but I didn't say anything.

She got out and sat on the front fender, crossing her legs like she was on a couch. I stood next to her and gave her a cigarette.

"So *that's* the kind of driving you do," she said. "Executive protection."

"I guess you could say that," I said, although I wasn't real sure what she meant.

"What kind of gun do you carry?" she asked me.

"I don't carry a gun," I said. "I'm a driver."

"Oh. What's your name?"

I told her. That's when she said her name was Daphne. I never knew a girl with that name before.

We drove off the farm. I followed her directions to a big apartment house.

The garage was in the basement. She had a different box to open the door.

"That's my space," she said. It had little walls on each side, I guess so other cars wouldn't bang into it when they opened their doors.

I backed the car in.

"You did that in case you had to get out quickly?" she asked me.

"Sure," I said. "I always park like that."

"Come on," she told me.

There was a little elevator in the basement. It only went to the lobby. We got out there. A guy in a uniform and a hat said "Good afternoon" to her, and called her by her name, with a "Miz" in front of it, like she was his boss.

We got in the elevator. She touched PH on the pad. I watched the numbers as we went up—PH was the top floor.

The room we walked into was bigger than a lot of houses I'd been in. It was all black and white, except for slashes of red in different spots—across the back of one of the chairs, on the seat of the couch, cutting across a lampshade. Even the floor was black and white, in squares. It kind of looked like a fancy bathroom, with a red rug.

"Would you like a drink?" she said.

I didn't know the names of the kind of drinks she probably was thinking of, and I didn't want to ask her for a beer, so I just said, "No thanks."

She went over to the bar to mix herself something. I looked out the window. It was easy—one whole wall was glass. I could see there was some kind of a terrace out there, but I couldn't see how you could get to it.

She came back with two glasses. "Ice water," she said, handing one to me.

"Thanks."

"You're a wonderful driver, Eddie. Did you have to go to a special school to learn all those tricks?"

"No," I said. "I just pick things up on my own." I wanted to tell her that what I showed her wasn't tricks, but I couldn't really do that without telling her what it was used for.

She asked me a lot of questions. And she talked a lot, too. I guess I got lost in the sound of her voice. The sky outside got dull, then it turned dark. I didn't care—there was nothing for me to do until at least the next day. Nobody was waiting for me.

"Is this all yours?" I asked her.

"This apartment?"

"Yeah."

"All mine. Would you like to see the rest of it?"

"No, I was just . . . wondering."

"If I was married?"

"No. How come you . . . ?"

"What, Eddie?"

"You have this place. And that car. And you dress so good. You've got a great job, right?"

"I don't have any job," she said. "What I have is a trust fund."

"A trust fund?"

"Money that was left to me. I can't spend it all, but I can spend a lot."

"You don't have to work?"

"No," she laughed. "I never have to work. What difference does that make?"

"It doesn't, I guess. Only, with all this, how come you . . . ?"

"What?" she said again. Only she sounded annoyed that time.

"How come you boost stuff?"

"Boost? Oh, you mean . . . in the department store."

"Yeah. What you took, it couldn't have cost that much."

"What *did* I take?" she said. "Let's see."

She got up and went over to where she had tossed her pocketbook. She brought it back, opened the top, and spilled it all out on the couch.

"Hmmm. . . ." she said. "You're right. This is all very tacky."

"Daphne. . . ."

She came over and sat real close to me. "Want to hear a secret," she said, very soft.

"If you want to—"

"Ssshhh," she said. She slid into me. I put my arm around her. "Don't look at me," she said.

It was real dark in there by then, but I still closed my eyes.

Her voice was soft, but I could hear every word. "When I'm in a store . . . not all the time, but only sometimes . . . when I'm in a store, sometimes, I get . . . excited. It's like there's this pressure inside me. Stronger and stronger. I get very anxious. Tense. I don't think about anything else. I know, as soon as I take something, it will be like a . . . release. All the tension will be gone.

"But, after I leave the store, I never want what I take. Just looking at it makes me feel bad. Guilty.

"I wish I could pay for what I take," she said. "Not with money. I could just buy things, if I wanted them. Before, when you told me I was being watched, I felt like I wanted to die. I don't know what I would do if I was ever caught.

"I mean, I *have* been caught, but not caught-caught. Once, a detective stopped me, but I was still inside the store, and I told him I was going to pay on my way out. They couldn't do anything. And once a store girl was watching me in the changing room. They had a little camera in there, can you imagine that? She saw me cutting the security tag off a dress and putting it in my bag. She knocked on the door of the changing room. I let her in, and she told me what she saw me do. All in whispers.

"But she let me go. All she wanted was a kiss. That kiss, kissing her, it felt like a punishment to me. And that made me feel . . . good. Because I deserved it.

"I had this dream, once. I was in a store, and a man caught me. He took me back in his office, called me a spoiled brat, and gave me a spanking. I was crying. He made me promise to never do it again. But I knew I would. I knew I would come back to that very same store."

She was quiet for a minute, like she was waiting for me to say something. I do what I always do when I can't figure out the right thing to say.

"You think I'm crazy, don't you?" she said. "Taking chances? I always do that. Look at you. I don't know you. I don't even know if your name is a real one. You seem like some kind of a criminal to me. A dangerous man. Are you a dangerous man, Eddie?"

"Only behind the wheel," I said, thinking of that judge, from when I was a kid.

"Oh, you're precious," she said. She was laughing or crying; it was hard to tell with her face buried.

*L*ate that night, she woke me up. I was on my back, looking up at her. She was holding the silver box with the red ribbon.

"What's this?" she said. "A present for someone."

"Yeah."

"It's for *me,* now," she said.

She tore off the paper like she was in a hurry. When she saw the perfume, she made a little noise in her throat.

"Is this your favorite?" she said.

"I don't know. I never smelled it."

Daphne opened the top of the bottle. She put her finger on the top and turned it upside down. Then she patted herself all over. Behind her ears, between her boobs, on the front of her legs. She kept going back to the bottle for refills. When she was done, she turned her back to me, so I could see where else she was putting the perfume.

"*W*here are you going?" she asked me the next morning.

"I have to see someone about work," I said.

"Take the Lexus," she said. "I've got another car. Bring it back when you come tonight."

It took me a couple of hours to find my way to where I'd been staying. I had to backtrack over and over again, but I didn't want to ask anybody for directions.

I guess it all started when Daphne said I had to tell her a secret.

I felt myself go cold in my spine when she said that. In my life, only one kind of person wants to know such things.

"What secret?" I asked her.

"Not any *particular* secret, you dope," she said. "*A* secret, that's all. It doesn't matter which one. Everybody has secrets. When people share their spirits, that's part of the deal."

"I don't understand," I said. I say that a lot, to buy time. But, when I think about it later, I always see that I hadn't been lying.

"Didn't I tell you secrets?" she said.

"About stealing?"

"Yes!"

"I already knew that," I said. "I mean, I saw you when you were—"

"Secrets aren't about *what,*" she said, whispering. "Secrets are about *why*. Remember what I told you, Eddie? About feeling guilty? And being punished . . . ?"

"I. . . ."

"That was a *special* secret. You're the only one who knows. I never told anybody. Do you know why?"

"Because they wouldn't understand?"

"That's right, Eddie! Don't you have feelings like that? Feelings you know other people wouldn't understand?"

"I . . . guess."

"You know you do. Everybody does. Everybody in the whole world."

It made me feel good, to know that. It made me more like a regular person.

That was the night I told her about driving.

I could never explain exactly what driving was. I guess I shouldn't say it like that. Before Daphne, I had never really tried. She worked real hard at understanding what I was telling her, but I guess I wasn't making much sense.

"Remember I told you, about a dream I once had?" she said.

"About getting caught?"

"Yes. The truth is, I have that dream all the time, Eddie. Not just that once. And even when I'm awake. Do you have any dreams like that?"

"About getting caught?"

"No! *Any* dream that you have over and over."

I didn't say anything. I wanted to tell her. There was no reason I couldn't. I mean, it wasn't like I would be ratting anyone out. My dream wasn't about stealing, it was about driving. But something was making me not say it out loud.

In my dream, I'm standing in the dark, by the side of a road. Yellow beams cut through the night; a car, coming. I can't tell what kind, but it's low to the ground. The car is black. Not pitch black—the same black as ravens, with a glisten to it.

The car stops. I can't see inside, but I know there's no one in the driver's seat.

The car sits there, waiting. I know if I get in, I'll be driving for all eternity.

I never get in. But I know one night I will.

"I dream about girls," I finally told her. That was the truth, too.

Daphne smiled at me, like I'd done something good.

I was on a blue leather couch, in the room next to the black and white one, waiting for Daphne to get dressed. She had the biggest TV I ever saw in there. I was pushing the button to change channels. Daphne has a setup where there's so many stations you could never really get through them all. She said there's a way to do it fast, depending on what kind of shows you like to watch, but I didn't care—I was just passing time.

On the screen, a car came along the road. A black car, with black windows. I watched. It was a killer car. Not the driver, the car. That was the name of the movie, *The Car.* I'd seen it before. It was pretty stupid, a car with no driver.

Not like my dream. In my dream, the car was *waiting* for a driver. Waiting for me.

I didn't hear Daphne come in. "What kind of car is that?" she said, right next to me.

"A crazy one," I told her. Then I explained what the movie was about, as best I could.

"Oh, that's like *Christine*," she said.

"Who's Christine?"

"*Christine* is the name of a book," she told me. "It's about a car that's possessed by an evil spirit."

"What kind of car?" I asked her, just like she'd asked me. I wanted to see what she said, so I could say it myself, if anyone ever asked me about that movie again.

"Oh, I don't know," she said. "An old one. It was in the book. By Stephen King, did you ever hear of him?"

"I think so," I said.

"He's the biggest horror writer in the world."

"Oh."

"It was a movie!" she said, clapping her hands.

"What was?"

"*Christine*, Eddie. It was a movie. Would you like to see it?"

"I . . . guess I would. But if it's like this one. . . ."

"No, it's a *lot* better, I'm sure. Come on, let's go get it."

We went to a video store. They must have had thousands of movies there. You could buy them or rent them.

Daphne said the movies were all in sections, so you could find what you were looking for pretty quick. I looked for a section about driving, but there wasn't any.

"Just ask the clerk," Daphne told me. "Here," she said, putting bills in my hand, "buy whatever you want, okay?"

"I've got my own money," I said. "Plenty of money."

She took the bills back from me. Put her hands behind her back and looked down.

"I'm sorry, Eddie," she said. "I didn't mean anything. I just wanted to buy you a present, like you bought me."

I started to say I hadn't bought that perfume for her, but I stopped . . . she looked so sad.

"It's okay," I said. "I'll just look around by myself." I took her by the shoulders and turned her around. "You see if you can find that *Christine* one," I told her, and gave her a little smack on the bottom so she'd get moving. I saw Tim do that once with Merleen, when they were in a store, and Merleen had liked it fine.

From the way she walked off, I guessed Daphne did, too.

I found four different movies that looked like they might be good from the stuff on the package. When I walked over to the register, Daphne was there. She held up a box for me to see. It said *Christine* on the cover.

"I got it!" she said.

When we got out on the highway, Daphne wanted me to go fast. She opened her purse and took out a videotape. I couldn't make out the writing on the cover, but the picture was of two girls, without any clothes on.

"I couldn't bring this one to the register," Daphne said. "It would be so embarrassing, I'd just die."

*W*hen we got back to her apartment, Daphne showed me how to work her VCR, then she went off to change her clothes.

I was watching one of the movies I found—I didn't think it would be right to watch *Christine* until Daphne got back—when I heard her come up behind me.

"Let's watch this one, first," she said in my ear.

It was the one with the naked girls on the cover. When I turned around from putting the cassette in, Daphne was naked, too.

*C*hristine turned out to be a pretty scary movie. The car was a demon. A kid owns the car, but the car gets jealous of him and kills him. And even when his friends figure out what the car is, nothing they could do would kill it.

"Did you like it?" Daphne asked me, when it was over.

"I guess not."

"Why is that?"

I thought about it for a minute. Then I told her, "I like movies about driving, not about cars."

"Well, let's look at the ones you picked out," she said.

*A*fter a few days, I could see that the place where I had delivered the car wasn't going to come up with anything for me to drive out.

Daphne found me a room in a motel. A really nice one, but it cost a lot. I didn't say anything about the price, because I'd already told Daphne I had money, and I didn't want to look like I had just been making myself big.

It was when I was staying in the motel that Daphne got me my portable unit. I always carry it with me now, whenever I'm going to be away. It's a TV and VCR all in one. The screen isn't all that big, but I only watch by myself, so it doesn't matter if I have to sit close.

I usually went over to Daphne's in the afternoon. Then I'd come back to the motel real early in the morning, before it got light.

After a while, I got used to sleeping in the daytime.

Daphne's place was perfect for watching movies, but she didn't like them all that much. What I would do was read in the TV guide about a movie that looked like it could be good, and then I'd watch it for a little bit. To see if I wanted to tape it, like she showed me. Even with all the channels Daphne got, it was pretty slow work.

Back in my room, I had that VCR that Daphne bought me, so I could watch the stuff I had taped at her place.

There were a lot of video stores in that city. I spent time in some of them, just looking. Other kinds of stores get all annoyed if you spend a long time doing that, but the video places didn't care.

One store had a guy working there that knew a lot. I could tell, because people were always asking him questions. I didn't understand a lot of what he said, but I could tell he knew what he was talking about from the way everybody listened to him.

Even though it wasn't all that bright inside the store, he always wore sunglasses. And a red T-shirt with a black vest. His head was shaved, but I knew he wasn't a skinhead—his tattoos were all wrong.

I waited until he was alone, and I went up to him.

"Do you have any movies about driving?" I asked him.

"Car chases? We've got them all, my man. From the classics to the contemporaries. *Bullitt* to *Ronin*. Are you looking for any particular director?"

"Not chases," I said. "Movies about driving."

"There's all kinds of driving," he said. "*Grand Prix* was amazing. The original, I mean, not *Driven*. That was a Stallone remake. Bor-ring! If you want to stay with the classics, there's always *Duel*. That was a made-for-TV, but we have it in stock. Did you know Spielberg helmed that one? Brilliant. You know the *Bandit* series? As in *Smokey and the . . . ?* Burt Reynolds is a comic genius. It wasn't recognized at the time, but you look at *Striptease* or *Boogie Nights,* and you can see that *somebody* on the Holy Coast knew it all along. And there's a lot of cult stuff, too, like *Death Race 2000.* Everybody thinks Carradine, but Stallone was in that one, too, before he caught fire. Then you've got truck driving, crime—"

"Crime," I said. "You have any of those?"

Some of the movies he sold me were pretty good ones. But none of them were what I wanted.

One night, Daphne said she wanted to go shopping. I didn't say anything—I didn't think she was asking me.

"You have to come, too, Eddie," she said. "Only you can't go in the store with me, okay?"

"I guess."

"Eddie, don't you understand what I'm telling you? I need you to be outside. With the motor running, so I can jump in and you can take off, fast."

"What are you going to do?"

"You know."

"That won't work," I said. "If anyone follows you out to the sidewalk, they'll get the license number. And they'd have a real good description of you. The way you're dressed up and all, people will notice you. And remember you, too."

I thought she'd be glad I warned her. I even thought she'd be a little impressed. But her face closed up and her mouth made a straight line. "Never mind," she said. "It'll be fine."

I was in the room with the TV when Daphne walked in. At first, I thought she wasn't wearing anything.

"You know what this is?" she asked me, coming into the light where I could see her better.

"Yeah. Like strippers wear."

"You mean a G-string? No, those are hidden. In the back, so it looks like they're completely naked. This is a thong. You're supposed to see a little bit of color around the waist."

Daphne walked past me, real slow.

"See?" she said.

"It's black."

"How very observant you are, Eddie. Anyway, I thought it would be perfect to wear tonight."

"Why?"

"Because I'm going to be bad," she said.

"I can't just wait at the curb," I told her. "There's no parking there. If I hang around, some security guy's going to come over and ask me to move."

"Just tell him to—"

"Daphne, if you do something like this, the last thing you want to do is make a fuss, get people to notice you. Just tell me what time you're going to come out, and I'll be right there, guaranteed."

"Oh! Yes, that's even better. You act like you've done this before, Eddie," she giggled.

I wanted to tell her that I was a pro. And that what she was doing was just a stupid crazy game. But I didn't say anything except, "Not me."

*D*aphne said nine-fifteen. At ten after, I crawled the Lexus along the sidewalk, like I was looking for a place to turn into one of the rows. The parking lot was crowded with cars and clogged with people. When it finally got clear behind me, I stopped and opened the trunk, like I was going to load it up.

I was behind the car, watching the store, when Daphne came busting out, walking fast, swinging her purse, heels going *click-click* on the sidewalk. I slammed down the trunk, got behind the wheel, and pulled up right across from her.

She jumped in the front seat, said "Get going!" through her teeth, like she was afraid somebody would hear her.

I whipped through the lot, keeping it smooth. "Come on!" Daphne said to me.

People who don't know think a car's not going fast if the engine doesn't roar and the tires don't squeal. When we got out to the street, I gave her what she wanted.

"*L*ook!" she said, when we got inside the gate to her father's land. She reached in her purse, held up a little scarf.

"Okay," I said.

"Eddie, this is a Hermes. *Very* expensive."

"Ah," I said, like I understood.

"We made a clean getaway," she said.

It made me blue to hear her say it like that.

*D*aphne opened her mouth. She held still while I tied the scarf behind her head, like a gag. Then she pulled up her skirt and put one leg over me.

I didn't even have to pull that thong thing down. Just moved it over to the side.

"*N*one of them worked out for you, huh?" the guy in the video store said, when he saw me walk in.

"They weren't bad, but—"

"Oh, I'm hip. The fit is everything. Try me on it again."

"Try . . . ?"

"Tell me what you want," he said. "*Think* about it, then tell me."

"I . . . it has to be about driving. Not about the cars. Not a chase, either. I mean, it's okay if it *has* a chase, but. . . ."

The guy just looked at me, waiting. He was very patient. I guess because he was an expert, and he was used to people like me not knowing how to say exactly what they wanted.

"It has to be, maybe, the man's *job*," I told him. "But not like a truck driver. Or a racer. More . . . special. Like not everyone could do it."

"*Thunder Road*," he said.

"What?"

"*Thunder Road.* The greatest moonshine movie ever made. Robert Mitchum wants to. . . . Never mind, you take it, try it out for yourself, then let me know."

"**W**ere you in prison?" Daphne asked me one night.

I had always been afraid Bonnie would ask me a question like that. Or Bonnie's mother, more likely. But I could tell from Daphne's face that she wouldn't think being in prison was a bad thing.

"Yes," I said.

"But you're so young. Was it a long time ago?"

"Long enough."

"Did you have to be in handcuffs a lot?"

"No. Just when they arrest you. Or when they transport you, like to court for your trial, or to a different lockup."

"Did you hate it?"

"Prison?"

"Being in handcuffs."

"I didn't like it, but it wasn't so bad. And it never lasted long."

"I wonder what that feels like."

"Prison? It doesn't feel like—"

"Handcuffs. I have a pair. Very nice ones. They're lined in velvet. But I was always afraid of them."

"I—"

"Come on, Eddie," she said.

*I*t was about six weeks after I first met her that I went over to Daphne's for the last time.

"I need the keys," she said.

"What?"

"To my car. I need the keys back."

"Okay," I said. I took them out and handed them to her.

"Please don't be mad, Eddie," she said. That's when I knew what she was talking about.

"I'm not," I told her.

"You're not going to stalk me, are you?" she said.

I just shook my head. It had been bad enough being a fake getaway man; I wasn't going to be a fake stalker, too.

*B*efore I left that city, I went by the video store one more time.

"Well?" the guy said, as soon as I walked in the door.

"It was a fine one," I said.

He nodded like I was making good sense. I was glad he didn't ask me to explain. I had tried to work it out in my head, what I was going to say, before I went there, but I kept getting stuck. The guys who ran moonshine, they were real drivers. It was like . . . I don't know, a contest, maybe. If they got through, they got paid. If they didn't make it, they went to jail. But they weren't bad men, and they always had people pulling for them. Not because they wanted the money, but because it was their own people.

For those men, driving the moonshine, that was their job. Even the cops who chased them respected them, if they were good at it.

"I knew it!" he said. "I'm on your wavelength, now. I've been holding this one for you. *Moonshine Highway*. The perfect vehicle for Kyle MacLachlan—remember him from *Twin Peaks*? This one's a minor classic. Underrated and understated. Very *noir.*"

"Thanks," I said. "Thanks a lot."

I held out my hand for him to shake. I could see from his face he wasn't used to that, but he nodded like he always did, and gave me a good grip.

When I got back to where I was living, it was like the time with Daphne had just gone past without me realizing it. Like it never happened.

I had the portable TV and VCR to remind me that I'd been with her. But when I tried to think about that time, it was like trying to read a book through a Coke bottle.

I called Bonnie. Her mother said she was married.

"That was . . . quick," I said.

"It was to Kenny, her old boyfriend," Bonnie's mother said. "They'd been engaged once, but Bonnie had broken it off. Kenny's in the military. He came home on leave, so they had to act fast if she was going to go back to the base with him."

"Oh."

"I'm sorry, Eddie," she said. "Bonnie tried to call you, but you were out of town on that job. She thought you would have been back a long time ago."

"I got held over."

"Well, it wouldn't have mattered, Eddie. I wouldn't want you to think that."

"I don't think that," I told her.

Sometimes, we have to wait around for a few days before we do a job. So we can be close when the time comes. Laying in the cut, J.C. calls it.

Once, when we were alone, J.C. told me there was another reason. Nobody gets told the whole plan until we're all together. After that, nobody leaves, so there's no chance of anybody talking.

This one time, there were four of us in on it. Gus always works with J.C. He's an old guy; older than J.C. "Gus was in the war. Not that desert vacation," he told me. "The real one. In the fucking jungle."

Gus looks all soft, flabby even, on his face. His hair is rust-colored, thin on top, but he combs it over from the side and you can't really tell unless he turns a certain way. Most of the time, he wears a cap.

"Gus can make things go boom," J.C. said, the first time he introduced us.

"Virgil was studying on how to do that," I said. "So we could blow this safe we were going to—"

"Virgil was an amateur," J.C. said. "Just like that dumb cowboy brother of his. Gus is an artist."

I didn't say anything. I don't like it when J.C. says things about Tim or Virgil, but I never let him see how I feel. I'm trying to be a professional.

"Guys like that, they never think about anything longer than tomorrow," J.C. said. He was watching my face. I wondered if J.C. could read my mind, like Gus is always saying he can. "Their idea of planning a job is figuring out which way to turn at the first corner. Cowboys, they never last."

"It wasn't Tim's fault," I said. I wished I could have stayed quiet, but I felt like a chicken was pecking at my nerves.

"He didn't plan it out," J.C. said, like a preacher from the Bible. Not like you couldn't argue with *him*; like you couldn't argue with the truth.

I wondered how J.C. ended up in prison himself, being that he could plan so perfect and all, but I never asked him.

I know Virgil would have.

Besides Gus, on this job we had another guy. Kaiser. His work was muscle. This was the first job I had ever been on with him.

He was a biker, or something like that. It was hard to tell from his tattoos; he had so many they got all smudged together, especially on his arms.

Kaiser was always looking at his own arms, like he wanted to make sure they were still there.

J.C. was going over everything with us again. He always says, you can't stick to the plan if you don't *know* the plan.

"Speaking of plans, what do we need a wheelman for?" Kaiser said. "This isn't no bank we're doing."

"You never know," J.C. said. "You never know when you're going to need a getaway man. And a driver like Eddie, that's the best insurance you can buy."

"Driving's driving," Kaiser said. "I got a dozen brothers who can haul ass."

"Driving's not the same as sticking," J.C. told him. "No matter what happens, Eddie will always be there when we come out."

"Fuck, he'll be the *only* one there, way out in the boonies in the middle of the night."

"I know what this is all about," J.C. laughed at him. "For a Nazi, you're a real little Jew, huh? Forget it, pal. It's equal shares all around, like I said it was going to be."

"Equal? You're taking half off the top before we split anything."

"That's for the planning," J.C. said. "The other half's for the execution. You know how it's done. Your work, it takes a couple-few hours. But the setup, my piece, I've been working on it for months, already."

"What do *you* have to say, Gus?" Kaiser asked him.

"Me?" Gus told him. "I don't have anything to say. You didn't want to come in on this with us, the time to say so was before you got told all about it."

"I'm not saying anything like that," Kaiser said. "I just don't see why this kid should get a full cut just for being a limo service."

"You don't have to see," Gus said.

"**N**o hard feelings, right?" Kaiser said to me, later.

"About what?"

"About your share."

"I'm getting my share," I told him.

"Yeah, I know. I mean . . . you're not slow, are you?"

"If nobody's chasing us, I always—"

"I don't mean slow *driving*. Christ, what are you, some kind of relative?"

"Huh?"

"Of J.C.'s. You any kin to him?"

"No."

"Well, he sure looks out for you."

"I know."

"**W**hat's the point of having a getaway man if we're going to be in this fucking tank?" Kaiser said from the backseat.

"The point," J.C. said, turning around to look at Kaiser, "is that, where we're going, we have to blend in. The law sees this big old Jeep, they figure we're a hunting party. Deer season's open. We got licenses and everything. That explains why we got the rifles. And that's why we're dressed for the part. Understand, now?"

"Yeah," Kaiser said.

"It's all part of the plan," J.C. told him. "My job is to think ahead. That's what I get paid for."

The house was mostly glass, shaped like a triangle, with the point on top. It was set in a stand of trees. If you weren't looking for it, you would probably never see it.

"Some 'hunting lodge,' huh?" J.C. said. "Only thing that doctor hunts up here is pussy."

"You sure the cash'll be there?" Kaiser asked.

"Cash and gold coins," J.C. said. "This guy's been doing outlaw abortions for years. He won't do regular ones. Even comes out against them; says it's 'killing the unborn.' Pretty slick, huh? Who'd ever think he was the man to see if your daughter was six months gone?

"He's got a little place where the girls can stay, before and after. Full-service. I heard he gets fifty large for each one. And not a dime of that gets reported, so it can't go into the banks. He's all-the-way dirty. When he comes back and finds his stash looted, he's not even going to call the cops. This one is perfect."

"It's a decent-sized place," Gus said. "I wish we had an idea where he kept it."

"We've got all the time we need," J.C. told him. "And nobody's around to hear the noise."

*G*us went in first, around the back. When his flashlight blinked from inside the house, Kaiser took hold of a sledgehammer in one hand and a big pry bar in the other and walked over to the front door. J.C. was right behind him, carrying a toolbox.

I knew they must be smashing the place to pieces inside, but I only heard a couple of thumps every so often.

I couldn't leave the engine running; it isn't good for a motor to be idling for hours. I got out some cotton rags and sprayed cleanser on them. Then I did the windshield, the headlights, and the wipers, just in case. I'd already hooked up a toggle switch, so we could run without taillights if we had to.

I never looked at my watch once, but I knew it was hours passing just by how I felt inside.

*T*hey came out in a line. Gus was first, then Kaiser, then J.C. Gus and Kaiser were carrying tools; all J.C. had was a little suitcase.

When I saw them coming, I got out to open the doors for them. Gus turned around, so he was facing Kaiser. He put his tools on the ground.

"Don't get in the car, Eddie," J.C. said.

Gus took out a pistol. He pointed it at Kaiser's stomach.

"There's one behind you, too," J.C. told him.

"Hey! What the fuck is—?"

"Open your hands," J.C. said. "Let everything drop."

Kaiser did what they told him. J.C. took out some plastic loops and tied Kaiser's hands behind his back.

"Walk," J.C. said. He made a movement with his head for me to come, too.

They marched him back into the house. Inside, it was all wrecked. Holes in the walls, chunks of the wooden floor pulled up, furniture all slashed, guts leaking out. There was a railroad spike driven into the floor, deep.

They made Kaiser go over by the spike. They told me to go get a kitchen chair. When I came back with it, they made him sit down. Gus pulled Kaiser's arms up, then dropped them over the back of the chair.

"We don't have a lot of time," J.C. said to Kaiser. "Where are they?"

"What are you—?"

"Your partners," J.C. said. "Where are they? At the bottom of the private road? Back at our hideout? Where?"

"You are stone motherfucking crazy," Kaiser said. He didn't act scared at all.

"I am," J.C. said, like he was agreeing with him. "But this is just business. We need to know how to get away from your partners. We need you to tell us."

"This is all bullshit," Kaiser said. "You just don't want to pay me my share. I fucking knew it."

J.C. put one hand under Kaiser's chin, and lifted it up. He brought up his pistol, and moved it slow in front of Kaiser's eyes. Then he pushed the barrel into the side of Kaiser's neck.

J.C. held it there while Gus wrapped more of the plastic cuffs around Kaiser's ankles, doing it so quickly I could hardly see his hands move. Then he made a loop out of the plastic, so Kaiser's ankles were chained to the spike.

Gus stepped back a couple of feet. J.C. stepped away, too. Kaiser was staked out solid; no way he could move from there.

"Show him," J.C. said to Gus.

Gus reached in his jacket and took out a fat sausage, like you'd have for barbeque. He held it up for Kaiser to see, like he was trying to sell it. Then he took out a coil of copper wire and cut off a piece with a pair of pliers.

"You wrap it around like this," Gus said. "Couple of times, nice and tight, so it cuts off the blood flow." He showed Kaiser what he meant. The sausage bulged around where the wire cut in. Three ugly little blisters, ready to pop.

"Depending on how tight you wrap it, takes as little as fifteen minutes, to over an hour. But, eventually, the tip turns black. No blood getting there, that's what happens. Like the reverse of a hard-on. Or a blowjob from a vampire."

Gus smiled. His face stayed flabby, but his little eyes were like shiny, hard black buttons.

"And then it just falls off. But that's okay—the wire's so tight, you don't bleed to death. Like a tourniquet on a wound. After a while, the next piece falls off. One piece at a time. When it's all done, you look just like a pussy. A pussy having her period."

Kaiser's face got all wet and suety colored. He smelled ugly.

Gus took out a pair of thin rubber gloves, like you see nurses wear in the clinic. He put them on.

"When we're done, we're leaving you here for the cops,"

J.C. said to Kaiser. "It's up to you. If you don't want to go back Inside without a cock, you'll talk before it falls off."

Gus unbuckled Kaiser's belt. I turned my face away. I knew I was going to be sick. I wanted to be outside, behind the wheel.

"At the first turnoff!" Kaiser said. His voice was high and thin, like a sliver of glass. "Just past that stand of white birch. They're going to block the road with some big rocks."

Gus stepped away, slipped around behind Kaiser's chair. That seemed to calm him down.

"How many?" J.C. asked him.

"Five. There wasn't going to be any shooting. When the retard gets out to see what's wrong, they're going to swarm the car. I told them, you're a professional. When you see all that hardware, you'll just give up the money."

"So *Eddie's* the retard, huh?" J.C. said. "You think it was a high-IQ move to smuggle that little cell phone in with you?"

"I . . . I didn't have no choice, I swear. They've got my sister. They said, if I didn't—"

"If you have a sister, you've been fucking her since she was ten. After your father got done with her," J.C. said. "Just thank fucking Odin or whoever that I can't stand a murder rap. When the cops get here, you tell them any story you want. But if you mention any of our names, you're a dead man, no matter where they hide you. Understand?"

"Yes. You don't need to do anything to me. I wouldn't—"

Gus stepped out from behind the chair and clamped his left hand on the side of Kaiser's face. His right hand flashed. There was a little thudding sound. When Gus took his right hand away, an ice pick was sticking out of Kaiser's ear.

I didn't take us back the way we came. I drove the car through the woods. The Jeep was perfect for that. I went real slow and careful, until I found a dirt track and I could make some speed. We stayed with the track until it dead-ended.

After that, we walked. Gus had a compass. We came out of the woods before first light, and I found a car for us in a few minutes.

In the morning, J.C. divided the cash three ways. "I'll have to put the coins out on the wire," he said. "Could take a while, cost us a few points, but it's the only way to play it safe."

Gus didn't say anything to that. Neither did I. J.C. wasn't the kind of man to cheat his partners.

J.C. went to get himself another bottle of Coke. He drinks dozens of them every day. Ice cold, right out of the bottle.

Gus was sharpening one of his knives. He's got a lot of them. Keeps them like razors.

When J.C. got back, I asked him, "How did you know?"

"About the doctor? He's a big man. With a big mouth. A

pussy hound, like I said. Man thinks with his cock, he's not thinking straight, Eddie. You never want to forget that."

"Not about the money," I said. "About Kaiser. How did you know he was setting us up?"

Gus laughed out his nose, the way he does when he thinks somebody's being stupid.

"I *didn't* know," J.C. said. "It was just a bluff."

"You mean, you weren't really going to let Gus . . . do that to him?"

"Nah. What for?"

"To make him tell—"

"That stuff never works," Gus said. "Not to get information, anyway. It's a crapshoot. I've seen guys take stuff make you toss your cookies just to *hear* about, and never say a word. And I've seen them die from fear, too, before you even get started. They go into shock, like—their hearts just stop."

"There was always that chance," J.C. said. "We knew he had the phone, but we didn't know if he ever used it. Anyway, you can't trust any of those fucking Nazis. A mutt like him, soon as he got squeezed, he would have given us all up, anyway."

J.C. took another hit off his bottle of Coke. "Some tools, they're only good for one job. When you're done, you throw them away, am I right?"

"Sure, J.C.," I said.

*T*hat was about a year and a half ago. The last job we did before this one. And this one, it will be the last job we do, ever.

"This one is our retirement score," J.C. said. "It all comes down to the odds. Percentages. No matter how perfect you plan, there's always the chance of a wild card being dealt. The wheels can always come off. You do enough jobs, sooner or later, you're going to get popped."

"You ready to go legit, Eddie?" Gus asked me.

"Sure," I said.

Later, I wondered about it. Wondered about what I would be if I wasn't a getaway man anymore.

"*N*obody's going home after this one," J.C. had told us. "Nobody's going back to tie up any loose ends. Nobody's going back to say goodbye. Everything you want to take, you bring with you, all right?"

That was why Vonda was with us. Vonda is J.C.'s woman. She's been with him a long time, I think.

Gus didn't bring anybody with him. Me, neither.

When I moved out, I didn't just sneak away in the middle of the night. That wouldn't be good at all—it's the kind of thing people talk about. I told some of the guys who hung around the garage that I was pulling up stakes, heading for California. Guys who like cars are always talking about doing that. I'll bet folks who spend a few winters out here talk about it, too.

I didn't have a phone in the house where I lived, but there was one in the garage. A pay phone.

I figured I didn't have to do anything about that phone, but I did use it to cancel my electricity. The propane man would just see I had moved when he came out next.

One of the reasons J.C. picked this cabin is because of the barn. It's in sorry shape. Probably hasn't been painted in fifty years. There's even big holes in the roof. But it's got good electricity running out to it, and there's enough space for all the cars.

J.C. has a brand new Ford Explorer. A blue one, with a trailer hitch for towing his boat.

"After this, I'm a retired businessman, Eddie," he said when he showed the whole rig to me. "This setup, it's perfect camouflage. Cops expect outlaws to move fast—only a civilian would be driving a rig like this."

Gus had a white Cadillac.

My car wasn't a new one like theirs. Mine was a 1955 Thunderbird. I hadn't been planning to put it on the road so soon, but when J.C. said this was the last job, and we couldn't go home after it, I hurried up and got my car ready to travel. The interior's not finished, and I haven't painted it yet, but it runs beautiful.

The Thunderbird was the only thing I wouldn't have been able to leave behind. I've had it for a long time. I still think about the way I got it, sometimes, because nothing like that had ever happened to me before.

The old lady who had the car for sale told me it was out in her garage, and I should go look at it for myself. It was jammed tight against the back wall, covered with a dusty tarp. There wasn't any overhead light in the garage, but the sun came in the open door enough for me to see what I was doing.

I only got the tarp a little way up before I saw what it was. When I peeled it off completely, I could see the Thunderbird had been sitting there a long time. The tires were all flat, the rubber on the windshield wipers was so dry it crumbled in my fingers, and there was orange peel on the rocker panels and around the headlights. The chrome was all pitted, and the floor of the trunk was rusted right through.

It wasn't locked. The interior wasn't so bad; but the seats had some ripped seams, and the dashboard had cracks in it.

The key was in the ignition, but I didn't try to start it up. It looked like nobody had in a real long time.

I put the tarp back on and closed up the garage. When I got back to the front door, it opened, like the lady had been waiting for me.

"Well, young man?" she said.

"It's a real nice car, ma'am," I told her. "But I couldn't afford to buy it."

"What do you mean?"

"Do you know what that car is, ma'am?"

"I most certainly do. It was my husband's car, Lord rest his soul, and it was his pride and joy. He was a minister, my husband. He used to call that car his little sin, because he loved it so. Kept it polished like a gemstone.

"When we'd go for a ride in that car, we knew people would be talking. A minister in a car like that, and a bright red one to boot! Certain as winter, some old nasty-mouths would be saying that's Satan's own color. But Hiram always said, his judge was the Lord, and he wouldn't answer to anybody else."

"Yes, ma'am. But, I mean, do you know what it's worth?"

"Well, there was another man come here a week or so ago, he allowed he could let me have a thousand dollars for it."

"That's a Thunderbird, ma'am. A '55. I could tell by the taillights. And I'll bet it's all original, too, just like it came from the factory."

"Oh, it is certainly not," she said. "It is in terrible condition, I'm sure. My husband's been gone, it'll be ten years this spring, and I haven't so much as washed it."

"No, ma'am, I mean, it's not changed from when it was new. It has the same motor and the same transmission and—"

"Well, that it surely must have. Many's the time the mechanic told Hiram he should get new parts for it instead of fixing up the old ones. It would be much cheaper to put a modern engine in, over the long run. But Hiram couldn't bear to have that. He just spent the money to keep her . . . he called that car 'she,' can you imagine? . . . running. Pride. Like I said, pride."

"Yes, ma'am. But what I'm saying is—"

"If you're going to be explaining things, you better come on in and have a cup of coffee with me," she said.

*H*er house smelled a little bit like lemons. She took me through the living room. All of it was wood, dark and light, and it all shined like new. There was a big Bible, lying open on one of those things a preacher stands behind when he preaches.

The old lady told me to sit down in the kitchen. She brought me a cup of chicory coffee, and took one herself.

"Now," she said, "what is all this about my husband's car?"

"It's worth a lot of money," I told her. "I don't know how much, exactly, but more than I could pay, that's for sure."

"More than the thousand dollars that other young man offered me?" Her eyes were brown. Bright and sharp, not filmy, the way some old people's eyes get.

"A lot more, I think," I told her. "There's places you could find out from."

"What places?"

"Well, I don't know, exactly, myself. There's magazines about old cars, for people that collect them, that would be one place. I don't sell cars; I only work on them."

"But you're sure it's worth more than a thousand dollars?"

"Ma'am, I absolutely know it is. There was this one guy, he had a car like yours—not exactly like it, his was a '57— and he paid twenty-five thousand dollars for it. Of course, his was all in perfect condition, but, still. . . ."

"Are you a Christian, young man?"

"I . . . I guess so."

"What do you mean, you 'guess so'?"

"Well, I'm not nothing else. You know, like a Jew or a Arab or anything."

"Are you a churchgoer?"

"No, ma'am."

"You mean you don't go regular, or you don't go at all?"

"I don't go at all," I said.

"Hmpf!" she said, kind of to herself. "I was sure you'd turn out to be born-again."

"I'm sorry, ma'am," I said. "Thank you for the coffee."

I got up to go.

"Hold on a minute," she said. "Would you pay a thousand dollars for my husband's car?"

"Ma'am, I already told you—"

"And would you want it to be driving it yourself, or to sell it?"

"If I had a car like that, I wouldn't ever sell it," I said.

"All right. Let me go and get the papers."

I was still trying to figure out what was going on, when the old lady came back.

"Here's everything," she said, handing me a shoebox. "My husband kept it all in the same place."

"Ma'am, I don't understand."

"My husband was taken by cancer, young man. It wasn't as bad as it sounds. His spirit was strong right to the end, and he died right here, in his own home.

"We had a lot of time to talk, then. A long twilight before

the night came. I got to understand my husband better in that time than in the fifty-four years we were man and wife.

"And do you know what he said about that car of his? He said, 'Ruth Ann, I want you to sell my little jewel,' . . . that's what he called it, sometimes . . . 'I want you to sell my little jewel to someone who is going to love her. Someone who will drive her around and show her off. Have pride in her. Not some merchant, now. And not somebody who is going to make a hot rod out of her, either. That's what she deserves.'

"Well, I said to him, 'Hiram, how in the world am I going to read a man's mind? You know how people will dissemble when they want something.'

"And he said, 'I've been praying over that one for some time. And the Lord sent me the answer. Ruth Ann, that little car is worth a lot of money. And that shall be the test. I want you to put my little jewel up for sale, but don't you put a price on her. And I want you to sell her to the first person who doesn't try and cheat you.'

"Well, I did solemnly promise Hiram, young man. But I couldn't bring myself to sell his car for a long time. I was frightened that I wouldn't be able to tell when someone was trying to cheat me—I'm not sharp in those ways.

"So I did what my husband did. I prayed on it. I didn't get a direct answer, but I was told that, when the right person came along, I could count on the Lord to alert me.

"And that's what happened. Every single man who has come to my house and taken a look in that garage has tried to buy my husband's car. Some of them asked me what I wanted for it, but I always said I wasn't sure. Not one single person ever so much as hinted to me that my husband's car was worth a lot of money.

"Then you come along and you say the truth. So I know you're saying the truth when you tell me you will drive my husband's car and keep it like it should be. Now, do you have a thousand dollars?"

"Not with me, ma'am. But I do have it. In fact, I have almost seven thousand dollars put aside."

"Never you mind that," she said. "You come back with the thousand dollars, and you take Hiram's car away with you."

Her bright brown eyes were a little damp, but she didn't cry.

I was jealous of Hiram, then.

The Thunderbird's still in primer, waiting. After I stripped the old, dull paint, I had figured on doing it in the original color—"Torch Red," it said in the papers that came with it—but, when I thought about my dream, the one about the car coming for me, I decided to make it all black.

It's the perfect car for my dream. It only has room for two people. They would even share the same seat; it's just a bench, not buckets.

Whenever I drive this car, I think about what it means to be a getaway man. Not just for a job, for always.

When this job is done, I guess I'll find out.

*F*or this last job, we've got a secret weapon. That's what J.C. calls him.

His name is Monty. I never seen him, myself. Everything I know about him, I know from J.C. and Gus.

The job is an armored car. It makes the run from the Indian casino every Saturday night. At four o'clock, so, Sunday morning, really. I never heard of an armored car that picks up at night, but that's the way the Indians wanted it, is what Monty told J.C.

J.C. said the Indians have all the power around here. The casino Indians, he means, not the ones who live on the reservation. Those ones don't have anything.

They keep the money in a vault with big thick walls. In between the vault and the outside is bullet-proof glass. Behind the glass, they have men with machine guns.

Nobody could ever get in there, J.C. says. But, sooner or later, the money's got to come out.

The way they do it is very slick. Every afternoon, an armored car pulls up to the casino. It goes around back where nobody can see, inside a special fence with doors in it, and another set of doors behind that one. Like the sally port the bus that brings you into prison goes through. After a while, the fence opens, and it comes back out. If you follow it, you see it go right to the bank.

The only thing is, there's nothing in those cars. They're empty. A decoy. The only time the money actually comes out of there is that night run, once a week.

J.C. knows this from Monty. And Monty knows because

he's the man who drives the armored car. An inside man, like Rodney and Luther had a long time ago. Only this time, it was different—everybody was a professional.

M onty doesn't drive the special night run every week. He told J.C. you never know when it's going to be your turn. There's a list of guys who they let make that run, and Monty's on it. He has to be by his phone every Saturday at midnight. They always call him, even if he's not picked to go that night.

The armored car company is real strict, Monty says. If you don't answer your phone even one time when they call, you get taken off that special list. There better not be a busy signal when they call, either. You're not allowed to give them a cell phone number; it has to be your home phone. And if they catch you forwarding the calls, you get fired.

Monty says you get paid for Saturdays whether you work or not, just for being ready. Real good money. And if they do pick you, you get a nice bonus. Monty's been there a long time, to get that high up on the list.

J .C. told me I couldn't steal a car for this job. What we're going to use, it has to be fixed up special. If you steal a car, you have to use it right away. The longer you keep it, the better the chance of getting spotted, even if you switch plates. Anyway, the car we need for this job, you wouldn't find one like it just lying around.

J.C. bought the car a few months ago. He always fronts the money for things we need on a job. That's part of the planner's piece, he says, the financing.

I've been working on the car J.C. bought for a few weeks now. "There's no hurry," he told me. "It's like a roulette wheel. If you wait long enough, every number's going to come up. And, if you *keep* waiting, that same number's going to come up again. The trick is not to go bust while you're waiting, see?"

"I think so."

"That armored car's like the wheel, Eddie. And every time they give the job to Monty, that's our lucky number coming up, okay? We don't want to jump the gun. If they call Monty out one week, and we're not ready, we just wait. They'll call him again."

It's nice up here. Peaceful. Sometimes J.C.'s around, sometimes he's not. When he goes away, Gus goes with him, mostly.

I never leave. Neither does Vonda.

She's . . . I don't know the right word for it. Not pretty like Bonnie was. I mean, she *is* pretty, but not the same way. Vonda has long black hair and eyes the same color as turquoise. She's real well built, and she's got long legs even though she's not tall. Her skin looks like she just took a shower, and her mouth looks like it was just slapped.

I don't think Vonda's much older than me, but she

knows a lot more. About all kinds of things. Vonda's smart. The only thing I know more about than her is cars.

So I like it when she comes out to where I'm working. Because she always asks me questions, and I know the answers for her.

Vonda found out about my movies by accident. Sometimes, when J.C. and Gus are watching TV at night— they like sports, mostly—I go out to the barn and plug in my VCR, and watch one of my movies. I guess I could just go in my room, but the cabin is kind of small, and the noise would come in.

I've got part of the barn all fixed up for when I watch my movies. I found this huge old armchair behind the cabin. It was all rotten from being left out in the weather, but I tore everything off, right down to the frame, and then I laid some pieces of carpet I found all over it. After I put enough layers on and wrapped it down tight with duct tape, it was real comfortable. You could even turn sideways in it, and put your feet over one of the arms, like a little couch. I made a footrest and a table out of some wooden crates, and I was all set.

We had plenty of long extension cords, but I didn't need any light in that part of the barn. I always watch my movies in the dark.

The way I have it set up, the VCR is in a far corner of the barn, and my couch and stuff are set up to the side. So there's a wall to my right, and I can still see if anybody comes in out of my left eye.

At least I thought I could. But, that night, first thing I realized was Vonda, whispering in my ear.

"What are you watching, Eddie?" she said.

I guess I jumped a little—I never saw her come into the barn. "Nothing," I said.

I pushed the button, and the movie stopped running.

Vonda came around the side of my couch. She was looking down at me. It was dark, but I could see her shape pretty good.

"I'll bet I know what you're watching," she said.

I didn't say anything.

"Don't be embarrassed, Eddie. All men like to watch those movies. It's no big deal. Some of them can be pretty hot, too."

It took a second, but then I understood what she was talking about. "No," I told her. "I wasn't watching one of those. . . ."

"Well, what *were* you watching, then?"

"Just a movie."

Vonda sat down. On the arm of the couch, with only half her bottom. She kept one foot on the floor.

"You wouldn't tell me a story, would you, Eddie?"

"I wouldn't . . . oh, you mean a lie, right? No, I'm not lying. It's just a regular movie."

"Where I come from, if somebody challenges you, you've got to show them your stuff. Do you know what I mean?"

"I guess I do. Like in a race, right?"

"Well, that wasn't what I was thinking of, but it'll do. So. Are you ready to show me?"

"Show you?"

"Show me the *movie*, Eddie. So I can see if it's what I think it is."

It was *Moonshine Highway*, one of my most special favorites. It takes place a long time ago, when people were better, I think. The guy in the video store had been right.

When Vonda had come in, the movie was near the end, where the guy in the Chevy goes after the guy in the Lincoln and they have their final duel.

I thought, as soon as she saw it wasn't porno I was watching, Vonda would go away. But she stayed perched right on the arm of the couch, watching until it was over.

"I'm sorry, Eddie," she said. "I never should have doubted you. I know you're not the kind of man who would lie to a woman."

"That's okay," I said.

"Well, it's *not* okay. I make that mistake, sometimes. Thinking all men are alike. But that's *my* mistake, and I shouldn't put it on you."

"It's all right, Vonda. I don't mind."

She looked over at where my carton of tapes was next to the VCR. "Are these all just regular movies, too?" she asked me.

*A*fter that, Vonda came out to the garage at night a lot. Not real late, and never for very long. First I thought she was trying to catch me watching one of those movies she thought I was watching that first time, but that wasn't it.

"I'm just trying to figure out what you like, Eddie," she said.

"Well. . . ."

"Don't tell me! I think I know. It's cars, right? I mean, that would make sense, you being an expert and all."

Nobody had ever called me that exact word before. I felt the back of my neck burn, and I was glad it was dark in the barn. But I had to tell her the truth.

"It's not . . . the movies aren't about cars," I told her. "They're about driving."

A couple of days later, Vonda asked me if I knew if there was any more of that old carpet I put on the couch. I said there was rolls and rolls of it up in the loft, but that ladder was pretty rotten and you had to be careful going up there.

"Can you go up and throw down a roll for me?" she said. "And is it okay if I set up in that corner way over there? I won't be in your way."

I didn't know what she was talking about, but I went up in the loft and pushed a couple of rolls of carpet over the edge.

Vonda worked hard for the next few days. She cut pieces off the carpet, then she hung them over a line and beat them half to death with an aluminum baseball bat Gus always keeps in his car. She washed down a section of the barn floor, then she scrubbed it with a brush. When she was done, it smelled like pine over there.

After the carpet was laid down over the section she cleaned, it looked pretty good. Vonda came out with one of those big radios, the kind that also plays tapes, or CDs, and has speakers on the sides. She was wearing stretchy black pants and a white sweatshirt. She had white sneakers on her feet, a white band around her head, and a thick pair of purple socks that went up real high over the outside of her pants.

She turned on the radio. A lady's voice said they were going to work on quads. Then the lady's voice said to do things, and Vonda did them. Different exercises. For each one, the lady's voice would count while Vonda did them.

It went on for about an hour. Every time I looked up from what I was doing, it seemed like Vonda was doing some other exercise.

"Now we're going to step," the lady's voice said.

Vonda went over and pushed a button and the voice stopped. She came over to where I was working.

"Eddie, I need a step platform," she said. "Do you think you could make me one?"

"I don't know what one is," I told her.

Once Vonda showed me what she meant, it only took a few minutes to make one. She carried it back over to where her carpet was, pushed a button, and the lady's voice started up again.

Vonda stepped up, then she stepped down. Over and over. Then she switched legs. After a while, she started doing things with her arms, too.

I went back under the car.

When the lady's voice stopped, Vonda walked over to where I was working. She had a big pink towel wrapped around her shoulders. Her face was all dewy from the exercise, but she didn't smell stale, the way guys in prison did when they finished lifting weights or playing basketball.

"That is *hard* work," she said.

"I guess."

"Men are always like that," she said. "It doesn't *look* hard, does it? Just stretching and jumping around. But it is. And it gets the job done." She turned sideways, stood on the toes of one leg, and pointed at the back of her thigh. "Feel that," she said.

I touched it, real light.

"It's real strong," I told her.

"*Squeeze* it," she said. "Come on."

I did what she said. I hadn't been lying before—her thigh was as hard as a piece of wood.

"See what I mean?" she said.

"Yeah."

"I do aerobics every other day, religiously. And I do my stretches *every* day. I drink eight big glasses of water every day, too."

"How come?"

"How come I . . . ? Oh, the water? It flushes your system. Keeps it clean. It's very important for good skin."

"Oh."

"Eddie," she said, with her hands on her hips, "why do you keep a car tuned?"

"So it runs good."

"It's the same thing with a person's body. You have to keep it tuned."

"I guess that's so."

"You wouldn't want your car to let you down, would you?"

"No. Of course not."

"That's because you rely on it, Eddie. It's something you need to get what you want. That's the way I am about my body, see?"

"Like a boxer?"

"Yes! That's exactly it, Eddie. Just like a fighter."

Sometimes, when Vonda was exercising, J.C. would come out and talk to her. I couldn't hear what they were saying. Not that I would ever try and listen.

Sometimes, she'd stop and go off with him. Sometimes she wouldn't.

J.C. came out to talk to me, too. About what we needed for the car, mostly. But he'd talk about the job, too, a little bit.

When J.C. would ask me questions, it was easy. When he stopped talking, like he expected me to ask *him* a question, it was hard. I'm never sure about things like that.

One time, Gus came out to the barn. He had some work to do, on the stuff he makes.

There was plenty of room out there. Gus put together a workbench out of sawhorses and some planks, but, when he tried it, he said it wasn't bright enough for what he had to do. So I took a couple of the trouble lights you use for working under the hood and hung them over a beam with extension cords. They dropped right down over what he was doing, and he said they worked fine.

When Gus was done, he walked past where Vonda was working out. I couldn't hear what he said to her, but I heard her say, "Get the fuck away from me."

When Vonda was done with her workout, she always drank a big bottle of water. Sometimes, she would come over and ask me if I wanted a drink. I never did.

Vonda was always asking me about my movies. After that first time I had told her, I thought maybe she'd think it was, I don't know, immature of me, or something. But she was real interested. And it was nice to have someone to talk to while I was doing things to the car.

She asked me when it started. With my movies.

I told her, when I was a kid. I saw this one movie. Not *at* the movies; it was a real movie, but it was on the television.

I had always wanted to see it again, but I never did—until Daphne told me all about video stores.

The Driver, it was called. I didn't know who was in it, but the star, the guy they called "The Driver," he was real handsome. Always very calm and cool, no matter what was going on.

When I told her about it, Vonda asked me if I had it on videotape. When I said I did, nothing would do but that she had to see it for herself. But I was . . . I don't know, kind of edgy about it.

So Vonda begged me. Not like real begging, just playing around. "Please, please, *please*!" she said, leaning down to where I was working. I thought maybe she was making fun of me, but I said okay. Only I didn't want to watch my movies in front of J.C. and Gus. I never did that. I didn't know what they would think.

She said that was all right. "We'll get our chance, Eddie," is what she said. "There's no rush."

Finally, J.C. and Gus had to go somewhere for a few days, to make sure about stuff for the job. They were always doing that.

The first night they were gone, Vonda watched the movie with me. I've been to movies with girls enough times, but Vonda was the first one who never said a word all the while it was on. Not one word; like the movie was important to her, and she didn't want to miss any of it.

And the minute it was over, she started asking me all kinds of questions about it.

Nobody ever did that before, either.

So I told her, the driver in the movie, he was supposed to be a getaway man, but he really didn't do it right. Vonda asked me, what did I mean? Asked me serious. So I explained. The man in the movie, when he had to do a job, he'd steal a car for it. That part was okay. But he never checked the car out.

You have to do that. You have to make sure the tires are good. Even the tire *pressures* are real important. The brakes, the shocks. You can be the best driver in the world, but if the suspension's no good, you can't make the car do what it's supposed to. You can't just grab something off the street and use it on a job right away.

Vonda never knew any of that. Her eyes got real big when I explained it to her. They had little black glints in the turquoise, like metalflake chips in paint.

It made me feel good, that she could see there was a lot more to my job than just driving for a few minutes each time.

So I told her other stuff, too. The chases, they went on too long. In the movie, I mean. It was like the driver had a plan that all the cop cars behind him were going to crash, and then they'd just leave him alone while he rode off. That's plain silly. It never happens like that.

The driver in the movie looked cool behind the wheel, but you could see he didn't really know how to do it—he was just acting.

Vonda told me the man who played the driver was famous. He was once married to some girl who was so beautiful she was in magazines. Vonda had a lot of those magazines. I thought they were J.C.'s, when I first saw them around the cabin. Maybe they were, even. But Vonda was always reading them.

*T*he next morning, Vonda cooked me breakfast. She always cooks, but she never eats anything in the morning. I thought, with J.C. and Gus gone, she wouldn't bother. But she made me a real nice omelette, with all kinds of stuff in it.

I went out to work on the cars we were going to use for the job. But I got distracted by the way the sun came in through a crack in the beams.

The sunlight fell right across my Thunderbird, and I felt bad, like I was not taking care of it. I had a set of headers for it that I was pretty sure would fit, but I'd never gotten around to trying them. I figured this was a good day to do it.

"*D*id you miss me?"

It was Vonda, standing behind me. Real close.

I looked at my watch. It was after three o'clock. I guess Vonda hadn't come out to exercise that day, like she usually did.

"I was working on the headers," I said. "I almost got it done. They're going to work perfect."

"Is this your car, Eddie?"

"Sure," I said.

"For real?"

"What do you mean, Vonda?"

"I mean, do you *own* it? Or did you just steal it?"

"It's mine," I said. Just for a second, I thought about the preacher and the sin of pride. I thought I knew how he felt. "I bought it, and I'm fixing it up myself."

"It's so cool!" Vonda said. "I think I saw one like it, once. In the movies."

"It's an original Thunderbird," I told her. "A nineteen fifty-five."

"That's as old as J.C.," she laughed. "Does it still run good?"

"It runs great," I said. "And when I get these headers all tightened down, it's going to run even better."

"Let's take it for a ride!"

"You know I can't do that, Vonda," I told her. "Nobody's supposed to see any of the cars we've got back here."

"This cabin's on thirty acres, Eddie. We wouldn't have to go off the property. Just a little ride, so I can see what it's like. Come on."

"Somebody might still see."

"From where? The road's got to be a mile away. And the woods are so thick around us. Just around the back, on the dirt path. We wouldn't have to go fast or anything. *Please!*"

We went so slow a fast runner could have caught us. I was a little worried about the undercarriage, but the ground was almost as smooth as a road.

"It's such a beautiful afternoon," she said. "Too bad your car's not a convertible."

"It is," I said. "I mean, I don't have the convertible part of it, but the top, this one, it comes off."

"Oh, do it! Come on."

"It doesn't just go back, the way a convertible does. You have to lift it off. Like with a hoist."

"But you *could* do it, if you wanted?"

"It's nothing special I'd be doing," I said, so she wouldn't think I was blowing myself up. "It's *supposed* to do that. It's called a removable hardtop. All of them had it."

"So we could do it, someday, right?"

"I guess," I said. But I didn't really see how.

When J.C. and Gus got back, Vonda said, "You boys have a good time?"

"We weren't there to have a good time," J.C. said. "After this job, we've got the rest of our lives to do that."

"Did you bring me anything?" Vonda asked.

"We've got to go again on Friday," J.C. said. "Tell me what you want, I'll bring it back for you."

Vonda turned her back on him and walked off.

J.C. looked at me and shrugged his shoulders.

"Do you like her?" Vonda asked me, the day after J.C. and Gus took off.

"It's just a picture in a magazine," I said. "I don't know her."

"I don't mean her personality, Eddie. Isn't she pretty?"

"She's not as pretty as you, Vonda," I said. As soon as I said that, my face got hot, and I felt stupid.

"How can you say that?" Vonda asked me.

"I . . . don't know."

"Look at the picture, Eddie. Now look at me. What's the difference?"

"She's a blonde, and—"

"And she doesn't have any clothes on. So how could you say I'd be as pretty as her?"

"I could just tell," I said.

Vonda's eyes got smaller for a second. Then she just reached down to her waist and hauled her sweater up over her head.

"Watch!" she said.

She took a deep, deep breath, and made her back curve. Standing just like the girl in the picture. Her boobs stuck way out, like they were going to pop loose from her bra.

"*Now* you can tell," she said.

For this job, there's two cars I have to get ready. One isn't a car, really; it's a truck. Not a pickup—this one has the back all closed up, like those yellow ones you can rent if you want to move your stuff. But I didn't have to do much of anything to it, really. Just check it over, make sure everything's working right.

The other car, the one J.C. bought, that's special. It's a big black Cadillac. Kind of an old one, but that's right for what its job is. It's a hearse. Not the open kind that carries the flowers in the back; this is the one for the coffins.

I put a lot of time in on that big hearse. We need it for the way it looks and all. But if things go wrong, it will have to be our getaway car, too.

*E*very time J.C. and Gus went away, Vonda would watch movies with me.

One night, she didn't come.

The next morning, she didn't make me breakfast, either.

I went out to the barn to work on the hearse.

She came out to do her workout. When she was finished, she came over to where I was.

"Did you miss me?" she said.

"I figured you wanted to watch the TV. I mean, in the cabin, not the movies."

"You didn't figure, maybe I was sick?"

"No, Vonda. I mean. . . ."

"You know I love to watch your movies with you, Eddie. If I don't come to be with you, there's a good reason. There's always a good reason. Okay?"

It made me feel all different ways when she said that. Like I was driving real fast, right at a fork in the road, and I didn't have a plan. But I just said "Okay" back, like she wanted me to.

J.C. came back from his trip alone. I didn't know where Gus was. J.C. asked me, could I have everything ready three weeks from Saturday? I told him I guessed so, but I would rather have more time, if I could.

I didn't look at him when I said that. I was afraid he would see it on my face. That once we did the job, we'd split up, and I'd never see Vonda again.

I think that's when he started hitting her. I heard him late that night. Right through the wall. "You stupid bitch," then the slap. I didn't know what to do.

I closed my eyes and tried to think about something else.

He was gone the next morning. I was working on the hearse when Vonda came out.

"You heard?" she said.

"Huh?" I said. That's what I always say when I don't know what to say.

"I know you heard, Eddie. It's okay. J.C.'s got a bad temper, you know. It doesn't mean anything."

I kept my head down. In prison, one of the things J.C. was famous for was never losing his temper. Guys called him an iceman—it was high respect.

"It was my fault, Eddie," Vonda said. "J.C. told me I shouldn't spend all day sitting around on my fat ass, and I mouthed off to him."

"You don't. . . ."

"Don't what, Eddie?"

"You don't sit around all day. You always make breakfast, and you keep the house all nice and you—"

She bit her lower lip and looked sad. "Oh, now I'm disappointed."

"Why, Vonda? What did I say?"

"It's what you *didn't* say, dopey. What you were *supposed* to say is, 'You don't have a fat ass, Vonda. Yours is just perfect.' You think I do all those workouts to be fat?"

"I didn't mean to—"

"Come on, Eddie. Tell me the truth. You *do* think I have a fat ass, don't you?" she said.

"I never—"

"Tell me the truth!" she said, like she was mad. She bent all the way over, so she was touching her toes. She was wearing little white shorts, and they rode up on her. She looked at me from upside down, her long black hair trailing down to the ground. "Well?"

"No, you're not fat, Vonda. You're . . . perfect, is what you are. I swear."

She straightened up, came over to where I was working on the axle. She kissed me. On the cheek. "You're so sweet, Eddie. I feel much better now," she said.

I knew things had gone wrong, then. But I couldn't stop myself from watching her as she walked away.

We watched some of my movies that night. I showed Vonda where they went off the track. Where they stopped being real.

J.C. came back the next morning. Vonda was real nice to him, fetching him his ice-cold Cokes, and rubbing the back of his neck.

J.C. had a big map spread out all over the kitchen table. He was sitting there, smoking. You could see he was thinking deep. Making plans. Every once in a while, he'd draw something on the map.

Vonda came over and tried to sit on his lap. "I'm working," he said.

"Oh come on," Vonda said.

He pushed her away and said something mean to her.

I went out to the barn that night. I was going to fix up the little drapes that cover the back window of the hearse so they stayed closed, but I ended up watching one of my movies instead.

Vonda never came, not even for a minute.

Late that night, J.C.'s voice came right through the wall.

"What the fuck is *wrong* with you?" I heard him say.

I couldn't hear what Vonda said back, but I could hear the hitting.

In the morning, he was gone again. Gus still hadn't come back.

We were watching one of the movies, when Vonda started to cry. I asked her what was the matter—it wasn't a sad movie.

She wouldn't tell me. I kept after her. Finally, she said that J.C. was really hurting her. She was terrified of him.

I didn't know what to say. I wasn't thinking it was okay to slap her around or anything like that, but I couldn't see why she would be so scared, all of a sudden. She'd been with J.C. a long time, I knew. And, in the daytime, it always seemed like they had made up.

That's when she showed me. The little round scar. She took off her shorts to show me, like it was the only way I would have believed her. I would have believed her, no matter what she said.

Way high up on the inside of her leg, right next to her . . . where it was so soft and tender.

I got sick thinking of the vicious red tip of J.C.'s cigarette, making her hurt.

I kissed where the scar was. She put her hands in my hair and pulled my head up. Then she kissed me, hard.

The next night, she told me the scar was old. J.C. had done it a long time ago. But he always told her he'd do it again if she ever crossed him. The next time, it would be one of her nipples, he told her.

"Right here," she said.

I closed my eyes. I looked down, so she wouldn't see what I was doing. But she must have figured it out.

"Look!" she said. "J.C. says it wouldn't be so bad, since they're nothing but fakes."

"Fakes?"

"My boobs," she said, so soft I almost didn't hear her. "You know what implants are, don't you, Eddie?"

"I guess I do."

"I didn't do that just to make them bigger," she said. "When I was a kid, the people who raised me never gave me enough food. Some days, all I got was laundry starch and water. It makes your belly swell up, like you're pregnant, so you don't get hungry. But it's not real food. That's no nutrition.

"That's what I had. Malnutrition. It's like when you almost starve to death. It sucks all the fat out of your body. Didn't you ever see pictures of kids like that on TV?"

"Like in Africa?"

"Just like that. Only, people here get it, too. Some people, anyway."

"Why didn't they—?"

"I got taken away from those people. And they put me in a different place. It wasn't so great, but there was plenty of food.

"And when I got bigger . . . older, I mean, my boobs never grew. They were just these sad little droopy lumps on my chest. As soon as I could save the money, I went and got the implants.

"You know what the doctor told me, Eddie? He said, now I look just like I *should* have looked, if I hadn't had that malnutrition when I was a kid. I could have gone a lot bigger, like some of the girls do, but I wanted to look natural."

"They look perfect, Vonda," I said. "Nobody could tell in a million years." It was the truth.

"They don't look perfect to J.C.," she said. "He's always saying I'm a freak."

"But you look—"

"There's a little packet in there," she said. "They put it

right over the muscle. J.C. says it feels like a sac of water. He doesn't like to touch me there."

"I don't. . . ."

"Eddie, tell me."

"Tell you what?"

"Do they feel like that to you? Like sacs of water?"

"Vonda. . . ."

"Just *tell* me," she said. She was crying.

I reached over to her. Even with my eyes closed, my hand went right to where she wanted.

"They feel perfect," I told her.

"You swear?"

"No one could ever tell," I said.

That wasn't true, but I guess I fooled her, because she stopped crying.

"I hate him," she told me, the next morning. It felt strange to talk about J.C. in the cabin. The cabin was like J.C.'s place. The barn, that was my place.

"Why don't you leave?" I asked her. "Go someplace else. Plenty of guys would be—"

"I'd be too afraid," she said. "You know J.C. How . . . dedicated he gets to things. He'd find me, no matter where I went. I don't have any money. I'd have to go back to dancing. And you can't do that with a bag over your head. He has pictures of me. Somebody would spot me for him."

"This job . . . the one we're going to do . . . there'll be a *lot* of money, Vonda," I told her. "With your share, you could—"

"My *share*?" she laughed at me. Only it wasn't funny, the way she did it. "I never get a *share*, Eddie. I only get what J.C. gives me. When *he* wants to. You understand? It's like he's got a chain around my ankle."

"**W**e don't have to t.c.b. on the spot," J.C. said to Gus. "He's got no moves. He doesn't know where we're going when it's done, and he doesn't know about this place at all. He's got to lay up at wherever he runs to, and wait for us to contact him at the number so he can pick up his share."

"It's fucking amazing amateurs live as long as they do," Gus said, shaking his head.

"**A**re you going to take all your tapes along when you go, Eddie?" Vonda asked me a couple of nights later, when J.C. and Gus were gone again.

"Sure," I said. "I've got a lot of them, maybe, but they don't take up much room."

"But your car's so little."

"The trunk's bigger than it looks. And I can put a lot of stuff next to me in front, too."

"That's not such a good idea," Vonda said.

"Why not?"

"Sometimes, you can't have everything you want. You have to pick and choose. Let's play a game."

"What game?"

"If you could only take one movie, just one, which one would it be?"

I didn't even have to think about it. I went and got my copy of *Vanishing Point,* and plugged it into the VCR.

Vonda watched the whole thing with me. Without saying a word, like always. Only this time, she held my hand.

When it was over, she said, "Why that one, Eddie? Why is that one your favorite of all?"

I tried to tell her, but I think I got all confused. *Vanishing Point* is about a driver. A great driver, driving against people trying to catch him. All over the country. He's not a robber or anything. Just a driver. And everybody knows he's running, because there's a guy on the radio who's on his side. So the driver can listen to the radio himself, and the guy who likes him can tell him what's going on. The cops are trying to get him, but a lot of other people are pulling for him, even regular ones.

"It's a perfect movie," I said to Vonda. What I meant was, it's not complicated, like *Moonshine Highway*. It's just the driver, driving forever.

"But he *kills* himself, Eddie," Vonda said, all upset. "At the end, he sees that roadblock, and he's speeding right for it. And he's smiling. He knows what's going to happen, and he's *glad*."

"No!" I said. As soon as I heard how my voice sounded, I apologized to Vonda. "I didn't mean to yell," I told her. "But you don't understand. He's not smiling because he's going to die. He's smiling because he thinks he's going to make it."

"But there was no room," she said. "How could he possibly—?"

"He was a great driver," I said. "He had a chance."

Vonda was real quiet for a minute. Like she was thinking over what I said.

"That's what I want," she said. "A chance. A real chance."

"You know what's wrong with that movie?" Vonda said to me in the morning. "He was all alone. He should have had a girl with him; *then* it would be perfect."

I'd never thought about that.

"He might have made it, then," Vonda said.

She reached over and held my hand.

Every time J.C. came back with Gus, they would go over the job again. J.C. is real careful. That's why we never got caught, I know.

"You want to hear the whole plan, Eddie?" J.C. asked me one day.

"Sure," I said.

When J.C. and Gus explained it to me, I was real impressed. It was so good a plan, the cops would never even figure out what happened.

The reason they told me the whole plan was, this time, I

had to do more than drive. I had another job. Scouting, J.C.
called it.

"You want a woman to fall in love with you, you have to
know what to do," Vonda told me. "You have to have
some techniques."

"What do you mean?"

"You have girlfriends, right, Eddie?"

"Well, I've *had* girlfriends. I mean, you know, girls
who. . . ."

"Sure. Did any of them really love you?"

"I don't know," I said. "I don't guess they did."

"You're the nicest guy I ever met, Eddie," she said. "But
if you want a girl to fall deep in love with you, that's not
enough."

"What do you mean?"

"There's little . . . tricks. Ways to act. I'll tell you one,"
she said, in that secret voice she has, sometimes. "You
want to get a girl to treat you special, take her shopping for
shoes."

"Huh?"

"Take her to the fanciest shoe store in town; tell her to
pick out whatever she wants. I promise you, she'll wet her
panties right there in the store."

"Did anyone ever—?"

"J.C. did, once," she said, like she knew what I was going
to ask her. "But he hasn't in a long time. He's not what I
need, now."

I wondered what would have happened if I had taken Bonnie shopping for shoes. If I hadn't gotten lost with Daphne.

"What *do* you need, Vonda?" I asked her.

Her eyes held me. I watched them turn a darker green. "I need a getaway man, Eddie," she said.

"Take her with you," J.C. told me.

"Vonda?"

"You see any other broads around here? A cop spots you driving around, doing nothing, he could decide he wants to stick his nose in. But he sees you with a woman, he'll think you're looking for a good spot to pull over and get some."

"If it's okay with Vonda. . . ."

"It'll be okay with her," J.C. said.

"It's the only place I can get what I need," Gus said to J.C. "Ordnance like that, it doesn't fall off a truck. And I'm not dealing with some fucking clerk off the base. These are people I did business with before."

"We'll be back in a few days," J.C. said to Vonda. "Keep your eye on Eddie."

He gave her a hard smack on the bottom. I could see Vonda's face over his shoulder; she didn't like it.

The days got filled, then. When I wasn't doing my scouting, I was working on the cars. The truck and the hearse, I mean. Once in a while, on my Thunderbird.

Vonda was with me almost all the time. Telling me about how to be with girls. Or watching movies with me.

One time, she even cleaned the Thunderbird. Real close cleaning, like it was a pot she was scrubbing.

It took her a few hours, working hard. "That was my workout for today," she said.

I told her the Thunderbird looked new inside.

"See," she said, "I'm good for *some* things."

"Vonda, you're—"

She put two fingers on my lips to keep me quiet. Then she ran off, back to the cabin.

That night, she asked me to bring my VCR into the cabin, so we could watch the movies there.

I liked it better in the barn, but she looked like it would mean a lot to her, and I didn't want to disappoint her.

When the movie was over, she went into the bathroom. When she came out, all she had on were a pair of her high heels. Red ones.

I couldn't say anything.

"Eddie," she said, real soft. "Remember when I showed you my scar? From the cigarette? Remember when you kissed it? That was a sweet thing to do. It's a sweet place to kiss. If I asked you *real* nice, would you do it again?"

From then on, Vonda was my girl. My secret girl.

"You sure it'll all go up?" J.C. asked Gus, after they had been back for a couple of days.

"A drop like that? Guaranteed," Gus told him. "Be nothing left but some bone fragments, if that."

"It's *all* got to burn. Otherwise, they'll keep looking."

"It's a hundred to one, with a full tank of gas, that it'll happen just from the impact," Gus said. "But what we picked up makes it a sure thing. Even if they find traces, they'll figure we brought the stuff with us to blow the box, in case the drivers didn't give over when we threw down on them."

He looked sideways at me and winked. "Yeah," he said. "I finally get some use out of what they taught me."

Gus meant the army. He talks about that a lot. He hadn't liked it there; that's where something happened to one side of his face. His right eyebrow is split in half, like he has two of them over just the one eye.

But even though Gus says he hated the army, it never sounded so bad to me, when he talked about it.

I wanted to ask him questions, but I never did. I'm always afraid of sounding stupid, but that wasn't it. With a man like Gus, it's better if he doesn't think you're too interested in anything about him.

*I*t was great riding with Vonda, even if I couldn't show her how good a driver I was. J.C. said to be extra careful not to attract any attention. Mostly, I just went over the different routes, and Vonda wrote down the mileage and kept time.

One day, Vonda slid next to me on the seat. She put her left hand on the inside of my right thigh. Not grabbing me or anything, just holding it there.

Right then, I thought about us just taking off. Just go from there. Drive.

But I didn't have a real plan. And Vonda deserved a better chance than just trying to run a roadblock.

*W*hen they told me how we were going to make the plan work—"selling the scam," J.C. called it—I got a little spooked.

Gus could see it in my face, and he laughed at me. "They don't bite, Eddie," he said.

Getting the bodies turned out to be easy. It was the first time we used the hearse. I was the driver. Late one night, we went to this cemetery J.C. knew about. It was a long drive, because he said we couldn't do it close to our base.

After we put the dirt and sod back, it still didn't look that good, even in the dark, I didn't think. But J.C. said it was a cemetery for people who died broke, and nobody would be visiting their graves.

That's when I figured out why J.C. and Gus had brought back that giant freezer from one of their trips away. After we put the bodies inside, I helped chop up the coffins. Then we burned everything.

"**H**ow come I never see you with a gun, Eddie?" Vonda asked me one day.

"I don't know anything about guns," I said. "Anyway, that's not what I do, guns. I'm the driver."

"J.C. and Gus always have guns on them," Vonda said.

"Sure."

"Don't you ever worry . . . ? I mean, if something happened. If you got into trouble and you *needed* a gun, what would you do?"

"I'd drive," I told her. "I'd drive everyone out of trouble."

I didn't see Vonda for all the rest of that day. At night, I went out to the barn to watch my movies, but she didn't come.

I was polishing the Cadillac the next morning when Vonda came up to me. She was wearing her exercise clothes, but she hadn't started yet.

"What difference does it make if it's so shiny?" she asked me.

"It's supposed to look like it's out on business," I said. "J.C. says, in this part of the country, folks sometimes have their funerals at dawn, soon as it gets light. So if anyone sees a hearse driving at four in the morning, they'll think it's on its way to a graveyard, somewhere."

"J.C. thinks of everything," Vonda said.

I could tell from her voice something was wrong. It was just a little tone laid over the top of what she was saying, but I knew Vonda real well, and I picked up on things like that.

"What's the matter?" I asked her.

"J.C. thinks of every*thing*," she said. "But he doesn't think of every*one*. Do you understand, Eddie?"

I could tell this wasn't any time to be saying I did when I didn't, the way I do, sometimes. "No," I said.

Vonda looked over her shoulder, back at where the cabin was. Then she looked at me, like she was waiting for me to say something more.

After a little bit, she reached around me to where my pack of cigarettes was, and took one for herself.

"Don't light that here," I told her.

"Why not? *You* smoke in here."

"Not this close to where I'm working. You see that carburetor over there? It's the old one off my T-bird. I'm soaking it in stuff that would go right up if a spark hit it."

"I thought you said you put a new one in it."

"Well, I did. And it works fine. But that one there is the original, and I thought I'd like to save it. So I'm getting all the gunk out before I rebuild it."

She made a little noise.

"You can smoke over by where I watch movies, Vonda. I'll come over and have one with you, okay?"

"Not now," she said. "If J.C. wanders on out here, I want it to look like you were working on the car and I just stopped to say hello. If he sees us over by your couch, he's going to get ideas. And when J.C. gets ideas, I get hurt."

"All right. I can just go back to—"

"Eddie, listen to me. What I said before? About J.C. looking out for everything? I want you to think about that."

"I don't have to think about it," I said. "J.C. looks out for everyone with his plans. And I look out for everyone when I drive. That's the way it is."

J.C. and Gus took off again just after supper. Vonda went into the room she shared with J.C., and closed the door.

I went out to the barn. Not to watch my movies. I wanted to see if this idea I had for the Cadillac was going to work, and I needed to weld something up to try it out.

When I saw someone come into the barn, I took off the goggles I was wearing.

It was Vonda. She had on a pair of jeans and a pink top, one of those tube things you can just pull off.

She came over to where I was working. Her hair was in a ponytail, tied with a pink ribbon. She had a lot of lipstick on. Long silver earrings. "Let's go to the movies," she said.

I stood up. "Which one would you like to—"

"Not *those* movies, Eddie. I know where there's a better one playing. Come on."

Vonda got in the front seat of the hearse. Up there, it was just like a regular car, a big Cadillac. She slid over, so I could get behind the wheel.

"This is our own private movie, Eddie. Special."

"I don't—"

"If you trust me, you'll get a reward," she said. "Just trust me, Eddie. Close your eyes, and you'll see a movie in your mind. Just like we were at the drive-in."

She moved in close to me. I put my arm around her and looked through the windshield. It was so dark there that I didn't have to close my eyes. But I did, because I had promised.

I tried to see one of my movies, but, instead, I saw my dream. The black car pulling up. I knew there was no driver. I knew it was me who was supposed to be behind the wheel.

Vonda made a little humming noise. I felt her pull my zipper down. Felt her hand.

Vonda took me in her mouth. Not a kiss, like she had done before, but real deep this time. I closed my eyes tighter. She made that humming noise again, louder. I put my hand in her hair, but I didn't hold her head down.

When I let go, Vonda made a different noise.

She stayed there, with her head in my lap. Licking me dry, the way a cat does.

Her hair felt like ribbons of silk in my hand.

I kept my eyes closed.

Vonda pulled her mouth away from me. "You think I'm dirty, don't you, Eddie?"

"Nobody would ever think that about you, Vonda," I told her.

"J.C. does," she said. "J.C. thinks I'm a dirty little whore. He calls me that, plenty of times. And he's right, too."

"Vonda. . . ."

"He *is* right, Eddie. J.C. makes me go with other guys, sometimes. When he wants something."

"You mean, like a pimp?"

"No. That's not J.C. A hooker could never make enough money for a man like him. J.C.'s not a pimp. He's a man who *plans*. And when he needs information for one of his *plans,* sometimes, he makes me be the one who gets it for him."

"I don't under—"

"One time, J.C. and Gus wanted to hijack a shipment of computers. A whole truckload of them. But they couldn't be sure about the routes. Where the driver would stop off for a break, stuff like that. So he sent me in."

"Sent you in to the factory?"

"No, Eddie," she said, in a sad voice. "Sent me in to work on one of the drivers for that company. He used to come into this club where I danced. J.C. made me play up to him, so I could get him talking."

I thought about the doctor. The one with the gold coins. I wondered how long Vonda had been with J.C. If it had been her who. . . .

"That's not being a whore," I said. "It's more like being . . . a spy, maybe."

"Spies don't have to go to bed with the people they're spying on."

"Sometimes they do," I told her. "I saw it in a—"

"This wasn't a movie," she said. Her voice had gone from sad to sharp. "This was real life. And this guy wasn't a Russian spy; he was a truck driver. That's something J.C. always says: a man can't eat pussy with his mouth closed. And, once it's open. . . ."

"Why do you have to talk like that?"

"I'm sorry, Eddie," she said. Her voice was back to being sad. "It's not the way I like to talk, not really. It's just that being around J.C. and Gus all the time, I started to sound like them. Now it's a habit, I think."

*A*fter I was sure the truck was running perfect, I took it out near the spot where it was going to happen. J.C. says it's no good just measuring with your eyes; the only way is to take the thing itself and see if it will fit.

I drove the truck down into where we would be leaving it. And I was glad I had listened to J.C., because it *didn't* fit right. When I walked back out onto the road and took a look back, I could still see the truck pretty good. I couldn't

tell how it would look at night, but I knew we couldn't take
a chance.

Gus showed me how to make curtains out of branches
and leaves. You cut some branches that have some heft
to them, but they still have to bend, so they hold their
tension when you put them in place. Then you lay smaller
branches across, like a lattice. Finally, you weave even
smaller branches—ones with leaves on them—in between
the slots. Unless someone gets *real* close, it looks just like
part of the forest. At night, it would be impossible to tell.

Gus said to build the curtains back at the cabin, then,
when we're ready, we could move them in the back of the
truck. It would only take a little while to set them up.

"Where did you learn to make these things?" I asked
Gus. "In the army?"

"Where else?" he said. He was squeezing his exercisers
in both fists. They're just a pair of wooden handles connected by a spring. I tried them once. It takes a lot of power
to make them close all the way. I could barely do it ten
times with my right, and I couldn't hardly do it at all with
my left. Gus can do it for hours, so fast you can hear the
handles click against each other when he closes his fists.
"Just one of the many valuable skills they taught me."

"Why do you call them curtains? Because you can slide
them open?"

Gus laughed. His laugh is always short and dry. Not like
something's funny; like he's making fun of something. "We
called them that because it was curtains for anyone who
walked past them, see?"

I didn't say anything.

"You missed out on all the fun," he said. "How old were
you when you first went down?"

"Nineteen," I said. I knew he meant real prison, not the kiddie camps.

"I was a year younger than you when it was my turn," Gus said. "Only, back then, as long as your beef wasn't too bad, they gave you a choice. You could take the ride, or you could give Uncle four years."

"You could go in the army instead of jail?"

"Sure. Happened all the time. It was just the same, really. In the army, you know what they called guys who made a career out of it?"

"What?"

"Lifers," he said. "You see what I mean?"

"Yeah. But, being in the army, it's something, you tell people you did that, they respect you, right? Not like being in prison."

"Maybe they do *now,*" Gus said. "When I was in, nobody respected you. Vietnam wasn't a real war."

"But there was fighting, right? People died."

"Oh, a whole *bunch* of motherfucking people died, kid."

There were some parts of the job where the best you could do was look it over real good. When I checked those things, it wasn't really scouting. It was the part I was going to have to do myself, like practicing on the roads.

When I went out to check everything for the last time, I took Vonda with me. For cover, like J.C. said.

We parked over near where we were going to leave the truck. After I made sure everything was going to fit just right, we drove over to the place Gus had picked out for

J.C.'s trick on the cops: an old played-out quarry that hadn't been worked in years.

I pulled the car way off to the side, where you couldn't see it from the road, then I walked over and took a closer look.

The ground up to the lip of the quarry was all rock and hard-packed dirt. I came up on it real careful, just in case it got loose without any warning.

When I looked over the edge, I could see Gus was right. It must have been a thousand feet to the bottom, easy. Sometimes, a quarry will have water at the bottom, but this one was nothing but stone all the way down.

I paced it off a half-dozen times. There wouldn't be any lights around the night we did the job.

When I got back to the car, Vonda was waiting for me. But she didn't act impatient, even though she couldn't play the radio or smoke while I was gone, in case someone might take notice.

"That curtain thing for the truck is amazing, Eddie," she said. "You really did a great job."

"It was Gus's idea," I told her.

I reached over for the ignition key. Vonda put her hand on mine.

"They don't know how long it's going to take you, Eddie," she said. "Let's go back to where the curtain is. We've got plenty of time."

It seemed like it didn't take long. But when I looked at my watch, it was more than an hour later.

"We're really kind of late, already," I told Vonda.

"*Please*," she said. Real soft, like the first time she play-begged me. "I'll just run in and get what I want. It won't take five minutes."

Even though it was a video store, I didn't go in with her. I could never get out of a place like that in five minutes.

When Vonda came out, she was swinging a plastic bag in her hand. She looked so happy.

"I got you a present, Eddie," she said, when she got in the front seat.

"What is it?"

"It's a surprise. I mean, you know it's a movie, right? But *what* movie? *That's* the surprise. You have to take it with you, so J.C. doesn't see it.

"Put it in the garage with your other tapes. But you have to promise me not to look at it. I want us to watch it together, okay?"

"Sure," I said.

"What the hell are you up to?" J.C. asked me.

It made me jump a little bit—J.C. almost never comes out to the barn at night.

"I'm making something. For the hearse. Just in case."

"Just in case what?"

"In case we get chased."

"We're not going to—"

"I know that," I said. "But this won't slow us down any. And it could buy us some time. *If* we ever needed it. *If* it works."

"Show me," he said.

So I showed him the tank I had welded up, with the rows of spigots coming out the bottom. It looked something like the mufflers you see on those old Volkswagens some guys convert into dune buggies for off-road racing—that's where I had got the idea.

The tank was going to run across the back of the hearse, just over the bumper. I was going to fill it with ball bearings—I had a whole barrel of them, soaking in forty-weight. When I pulled the lever, the ball bearings would spill out behind the hearse. No way anyone chasing us could stay on the road when they ran over them.

"That's a sweet piece of engineering," J.C. said.

Even with all that had been on my mind, it still felt good when he said that.

"It's like you always say," I said. "If you plan for things to go wrong, they usually don't."

He gave me a big grin. Then he went back to the cabin.

Vonda came out to the barn that night. I was on the couch, but I was just sitting there, thinking.

"You didn't watch that movie I bought, did you?" she said.

"I would never do that. I waited for you. Did you want to watch it now?"

"No, not now. I can't stay long. And, anyway, I don't

want us to watch it out here. J.C. and Gus are taking off again in a day or two, for one last time. We can watch it then."

"Okay."

Vonda picked up my pack of cigarettes and lit one for herself. She didn't sit down. I couldn't see her face in the dark.

"When this is over, he's not going to take me with him, Eddie," she said. "I'm good for some things, sure. But, after this job, he won't need me for any of them."

"But . . . but you said . . . you said, if you ever tried to get away from him, he'd track you down, Vonda. If he doesn't want you anymore, why would he care?"

She took a long drag from her cigarette. I could see her face behind the red glow for a second.

"Think about it," she said.

"I *have* been thinking about it," I told her. "Only, this makes it different. Makes it easy. If J.C. is going to leave you, you can go with me. In my car. I'll split my share with you, Vonda. There'll be plenty—"

"You think it's that easy? You'll be in the hearse; they'll be in the truck. With the money."

"They have to come back here, Vonda. Everything's here. Their cars and all their ID and—"

"Oh, they have to come back all right," she said. She took another drag. "They have to clean up all the loose ends before they get gone for good."

"But if they—"

Vonda ground out her cigarette in the hubcap I used for an ashtray. "I have to go in now, Eddie," she said. "Just *think* about it, okay?"

The next day, we were all eating lunch in the cabin. The television was on, with the sound off. Gus liked it that way. He was squeezing his hand things. *Click-click.*

J.C. told Gus about what I was rigging up with the ball bearings. Gus nodded at me, like he does when I finally understand something he's been saying.

J.C. wanted to know when I'd be finished with the hearse. "A few more days," I told him.

Vonda and J.C. argued about something before they went to bed, but I didn't hear any sounds of hitting through the walls all that night. I guessed they had made up.

When I got up the next morning, nobody was around. I made myself some bacon and eggs. I don't cook as good as Vonda, but I do pretty good. Virgil always said he was going to teach me to barbeque someday, but he never got the chance.

I made plenty extra, in case they came out and wanted something, too. But nobody did. So I went to work.

I was in the barn when I heard the car take off. When I went back over to the cabin, J.C. and Gus were both gone.

It was after lunchtime, so I made myself a sandwich.

Vonda didn't come out of the bedroom until almost three o'clock. I looked at her face, but I couldn't see any marks.

I asked her if she wanted something to eat.

"Not now, Eddie," she said. "I have to take a hot bath."

Vonda was in there a long time. I didn't know what to do. I went over to the door, stood real close by, but I couldn't hear anything.

I knocked. Soft, but loud enough for her to hear.

I still couldn't hear anything. I opened the door, slow. In case she was. . . . I couldn't even say the rest of that in my mind.

Vonda was in the tub. She was crying, but quiet, like she didn't want anybody to hear.

"What is it?" I said.

She started crying louder, then.

I went over and held the back of her head.

It took a long time for her to tell me what happened. The reason I hadn't heard anything the night before was because J.C. had tied her up. He wanted to do something to her she didn't like. And he wanted Gus to do it to her, too. He put tape over her mouth, so she couldn't yell.

That's why she needed the bath, because what he did hurt so much.

She said, sometimes, J.C. and Gus had her at the same time. She said Gus liked to hurt girls, and J.C. let him do what he wanted.

I closed my eyes. When I did, I saw little red dots, like the tips of cigarettes.

"Wash me, Eddie," she said, crying. "Get me all clean. I have to get all clean."

She was so limp, I had to hold her arms up to wash

under them. When I was all done with her front, I said, "Vonda, do you want me to. . . ."

"I'm dirty, Eddie," she said. She turned over in the tub. She put her hands on the edge so she could keep her face out of the water, and I did her other side. "Scrub *hard,*" Vonda said. "Get it all."

When I was all finished, I helped her stand up. I got the towels and patted her dry.

Vonda turned her back, and said something real low.

"What, girl?" I said.

"Am I all clean now, Eddie?"

"All clean," I said.

She turned and kissed me. Not a sex kiss; on the cheek.

"I can always count on you," she said. "I'm going to get dressed now."

When Vonda came out of the bedroom, she had her hair in a ponytail, like she did before, and her face was all scrubbed. She was wearing a big white T-shirt that came down over her knees. For a second, a picture of Janine popped into my mind. I wondered if they had treated her good in that foster home.

"I want to tell you a secret," she said.

I sat down in the easy chair. Vonda sat on my lap. Not the way a woman does. All curled up, like a little girl.

"It seems, all my life, I've been looking for a getaway man," she said. "Even when I was a kid. Other little girls, they used to dream about Prince Charming. You know,

someone to ride up on a white horse and take them to a cas-
tle, where they'd be a princess and everything would be
perfect. Me, I always knew it would be a man in a car.
Honking the horn in front of the house. And I'd run out, and
go away with him.

"I ran to that horn plenty of times, Eddie. Only it was
never a prince behind the wheel.

"All my life, I've been waiting. What I told you before, it's
God's truth, Eddie. You're my getaway man. That's my half
of it, Eddie. The other half, you have to make come true.
Promise me."

I didn't tell Vonda about my own dream, because it was
already coming true. But I did promise her.

"I wish I could sleep with you," Vonda said, when I came
back into the cabin that night.

"Why couldn't we?"

"Not that, Eddie," she said. "*Sleep* with you. The way a
wife does with her husband. In the same bed. All night. So
when I woke up in the morning, you'd be the first thing I
saw."

"We can do that," I said. "We can—"

"We *will* do that," she said, in a fierce voice. "But we
can't do it here. Not ever. I don't know when they're coming back. I never do. And if J.C. ever caught us, you know
what he'd do."

I wasn't sure what he would do, but I didn't want to argue.

"But we could do something *like* it," she said. "If you're
willing."

"I'll do whatever you want, Vonda."

"Go sit on the couch," she said. "I'll be right back."

She was gone a lot more than a little while. I just sat there.

When she came out of the bedroom, she was wearing a black slip. Her hair was down and she didn't have on any makeup. Or any shoes. She looked real little that way.

"This is like a nightgown, isn't it, Eddie?"

"I guess it is."

She had a blanket in one hand. She gave it to me. Then she laid down on the couch, so her head was in my lap.

"Put that over me," she said.

I did that, and she snuggled into it so it was all wrapped around her.

"I'm going to sleep," she said. "Right here. Just a little nap. You can watch television; it won't bother me at all. Okay?"

"Sure."

"And, when I wake up, you'll be right there, Eddie. I feel so safe when I'm with you watching over me, I could sleep like a baby. I'll bet I have sweet dreams."

I stroked her hair, to help her fall asleep.

"Goodnight kiss!" she said, in a bratty kid's voice.

As soon as I kissed her, she closed her eyes.

I was watching a TV movie. The *Badlands*. It was about a young guy who killed a whole bunch of people. He had his girlfriend with him the whole time he was doing it. They drove all over the place, across the state lines and everything. But, when the cops got close, he didn't try to get away; he just gave up.

The girl was *real* young, just a baby who didn't know anything. The movie tried to make it out like she was as guilty as him. But I could tell she was innocent. He was a guy who just liked killing, and she didn't have any choice but to go along with him.

Vonda stirred in my lap. "Hi, honey," she said.

That was the first time she ever called me that.

"Did you sleep good?" I asked her.

"Like an angel," she said. "Eddie, could you do something for me?"

"Sure."

"Could you sleep out in the barn tonight? On your couch? I'm afraid, if I knew you were sleeping in the next room from me, I couldn't stop myself from going to be with you."

"We could just—"

"Please, Eddie," she said. "I know I'm being a pain, but, just this once . . . ?"

When I got up in the morning, I went into the cabin to take a shower. The room where Vonda and J.C. stayed was closed; I guessed she was still asleep.

I was eating breakfast when Vonda came out. She was wearing her bathrobe. It's white, and it looks like it's made out of towels. She had the belt tied tight, but I could see she didn't have anything on under it.

She went into Gus's room. I had never seen her do that in all the time we had been staying there.

She came out with a cigar box in her hands.

"This is Gus," she said. And she handed the box to me.

I opened it up. Inside were pictures. Girls. They were all tied up. But not like Daphne wanted to be tied up—these girls, it looked like they were tied up for real. And the way they were tied, it had to hurt. One girl, from the look on her face, you could tell the ropes were really cutting into her.

There was no reason to tie them up like that just to keep them from getting away, so it *had* to be like it was with Daphne. But I could tell it wasn't.

At the bottom of the pile, a girl was tied to a long, thick piece of wood, like a pig on a spit. She was facing the camera. There was a man behind her, but you couldn't see his face. Her eyes had a lot of white showing. Her mouth was open, like she was screaming.

"This is Gus," Vonda said, again. I couldn't tell if she meant it was Gus in the picture. I didn't want to ask.

"Careful," she said. "They have to go back in the exact same order, otherwise he'll know someone was looking."

I didn't touch them. Vonda stacked them, so it was like they were before. Then she went and put the box back in Gus's room.

I went back out to where the cars were.

I didn't see Vonda all that day. But we had supper together. She made a stew, with all kinds of stuff in it. I told her it was the best I ever had, and I wasn't lying—Virgil never made stew.

"Thank you, Eddie. That was sweet. Are you ready to see your movie now?" she asked me. "The present I got for you?"

"Sure."

"Well, go get it!" she said, smiling at me.

*T*he movie was *Rebel Without a Cause*. The cover on the box had a guy in a leather jacket, standing next to an old Mercury.

"It's not about driving, Eddie," Vonda said. "It's a love story. But it's my favorite of all time. And I wanted you to watch it with me. Is that okay, honey?"

I told her sure it was. Just because all my own movies are about driving doesn't mean I couldn't like anything else.

We sat down together and watched. The movie was about a kid who didn't fit in. He never fit in. His family just moved to a new town, and he didn't fit in there, either.

There was a girl he really liked. A pretty one, with dark hair. Only that girl already had somebody—the leader of the gang he wanted to be in.

The kid in the movie, he was trying to make the other kids like him, but it wasn't working. They wouldn't let him join. So he got in a drag race with the boyfriend of the girl he liked.

The movie went on after that, but it was right then that I figured out how to do what I had to.

I looked over at Vonda, to see if she understood, but she was lost in the movie.

She cried when it was over. I couldn't tell if she was crying sad, or crying happy. A kid—a little, scared kid; the best friend of the guy who ended up with the girl—he died at the end. But the rebel and the girl he liked ended up being with each other.

A few years ago, a guy brought his Mustang into my place. He wanted it to get off the line better. Not for real racing; just the kind of thing some guys do at stoplights.

I told him, he either needed more engine or a lower rear end. He asked me a lot of questions about changing the rear end, like he never heard of such a thing.

I went behind the car to show him something. He had a lot of stickers all over the bumper. I remember there was a couple of Confederate flags. And one that said, "WWJD."

I asked him what that stood for. He told me, "What Would Jesus Do?"

That confused me, so I asked him, how would a person know? He said, you just have to ask yourself the question. "What would Jesus do?" Then, whatever Jesus would do, that's the right thing. And you try to do it yourself.

I couldn't see how people could know what Jesus would do, but I didn't say anything.

Before, watching the movie, I was thinking I knew what I had to do. But the more I thought about it, the more I realized, just knowing *how* to do something doesn't mean you *should* do it.

What would Tim do? I asked myself, inside my mind.

J.C.'s the smartest man I ever knew. He's smart about planning and things like that. But Tim was the smartest one about doing what's right. Everybody said that about him. Especially after the trial.

I felt grief in my heart, because the one man who would know the answer I needed, I couldn't ask.

And then I was disgusted with myself for what I had been thinking. Feeling bad because I couldn't ask Tim was just another way of feeling bad for myself, not for Tim.

I never think about Tim or Virgil. Because, every time I do, I feel all empty and crushed, like a soda can in one of those recycling machines.

I used to dream—not a real dream, I guess, because I was always awake when I had it—of breaking Tim out of prison, the way I saw in some movies.

It's not impossible. People break out of prison. I heard, once, guys even broke out of death row, over in Virginia. I don't know if that one's true, but I feel like it could be.

I know Tim would try, that's for sure.

The guys who broke out in Texas, that whole bunch of them, they did it themselves, from inside. But, when they got out, there was a car waiting for them.

I could do that part. If Tim could ever get out, I could be the driver.

I didn't know how to do anything else. If Tim ever got word to me, I'd be waiting wherever he said. With the fastest, best car there ever was.

But Tim never wrote me a letter, and I never wrote him. I knew why Tim never wrote, and I wouldn't dishonor him by going against what he wanted.

I always read the papers, hoping. But Tim's name doesn't get in the papers anymore.

There's other ways to get out of prison I heard about. There's lawyers, people with connections, politicians. They can fix things. I don't know anything about that for myself, but everybody in prison says that's the way things are. What it takes is money. Heavy money, because it has to be spread around.

When this job is over, I'm going to find one of those fixers, see if he can do something for Tim. I'm not sure where I would look, but there's people I guess I could ask.

I kept thinking, the best person to ask would be J.C. I felt bad I couldn't do that, but that wasn't a selfish feeling. Because, that time, it wasn't me that I was feeling bad for.

I truly believed, if Hiram was still around, he would be a man I could ask. Not because he was a preacher, or because he'd know what Jesus would do. Because of the kind of man he was, to have his woman love him so deep, long after he was gone.

And she had picked me, too, to look after Hiram's car.

One day, I took the Thunderbird out for a drive. I knew I shouldn't have done it. But I just had to, even though I couldn't say why.

I didn't want to go fast, or practice turns or anything. I just wanted to drive. By myself.

The sun was bright, but it wasn't that hard white it gets sometimes. It was a soft, pretty glow, like it was coming through those big colored windows they have in churches.

The Thunderbird wanted to run, but I kept the leash tight. I found a good station on the radio. They had a Delbert McClinton song playing. He's one of the ones I like the best.

I came around a long curve, as smooth as water over river rocks. I was thinking those new shocks I had put in were really doing the job . . . and then I saw the cop car.

It was parked over the side, like it was waiting for speeders. I knew I wasn't speeding, but I kind of held my breath.

And then the cop car pulled out behind me.

His light bar wasn't flashing.

I knew the roads around there perfect. I should have, as much scouting and practicing as I had done. I didn't know what the troopers had in their cars, but I was sure I could lose him if I could get off the highway.

But, sooner or later, I would have to go back to the cabin. There was no phone there; I'd have to go myself.

And if the cops were watching for me, everybody was finished.

I didn't need to have Tim around to ask what the right thing to do was.

I slowed down and moved a little to the right, like I was letting the cop car pass.

The trooper swung out and came alongside me. I looked over at him—that's the natural thing to do. And he pointed with his right hand, telling me to pull over.

I did it. The trooper pulled over, too. But not behind me, the way they always do. In front.

The trooper got out of his cruiser and walked toward me. I rolled down the window and reached in my wallet for my license and registration. Even scared, it felt good, knowing I had all that, like I was a regular person.

"Where'd you get this?" the cop asked me.

"It's mine," I said. "I bought it from—"

"No, son. I mean, where in the world did you find yourself a fifty-five? You don't see one of these every day. You cherrying it out?"

"Yes, sir," I said. "I've been working on it for almost three years."

"Damn! Mind if I take a look?"

"My pleasure," I said. And I wasn't lying. I popped the hood. Then I got out and lifted it up for him.

"That carb's not stock," he said. He sounded a little disappointed.

"I got the original back home," I told him. "And the original exhaust manifolds, too."

"You going to put them back on when you're done?"

"I . . . I don't rightly know. I was thinking, maybe I would, someday. But it runs a lot better this way."

"I'll just bet. Cold mornings, I can sit there forever before I get mine to fire up."

"You've got one, too?"

"A fifty-six," he said. "Goldenrod yellow, with a white porthole top." He looked at the seats. "Yours was, what, red from the factory?"

"Torch red," I told him, proud that I knew.

The trooper walked around to the back of the car, but he didn't roll his shoulders the way cops do when they're trying to make you nervous.

"Are those the original skirts, or did you get them NOS?"

"Original," I told him.

"I've been looking for a pair for mine for years," he said. "I got the Continental kit, though."

"I saw one of those, once. On a fifty-seven. It looked great."

"Gives you more room in the trunk, too," he said. "I'm not one of those guys who only brings his car to shows. I *drive* mine."

"Me, too," I said.

"I know a place sells the original paint," he said. "They still got some in stock."

"For real?"

"Absolutely. When you're going numbers-match, it has to be all authentic, right?"

"Right. Where's it at, that place that sells the paint?"

The trooper stayed with me for quite a while. Long enough for me to smoke a couple of cigarettes. He even had one with me.

Finally, he said he had to get going. He said it was a pleasure meeting someone else who had an old T-bird to drive, not just to keep in the garage and only bring out on Sundays when it doesn't rain, like some.

We gave each other our names, and shook hands. He never asked to see my license.

After he took off, I kept driving in that same direction for a while, just to be sure.

I felt a happiness in me, like I had done good. I wished Hiram's wife could have seen me, representing his jewel.

"**Y**ou got her ready to roll?" J.C. asked me, at the end of the week. He was talking about the hearse; the truck didn't need anything.

"Pretty much," I said. "I still don't know where Gus wants to put that stuff of his."

"Don't worry about it," J.C. said. "Gus says it's no bigger than a little suitcase. Not like the damn money. That's all going to be in mixed bills, so we're figuring about two, three hundred pounds for every million. Going to be a lot of heavy little sacks. That's why we had to get the truck."

"I thought it was because—"

"Because the hearse isn't coming back? Nah. Look, Eddie, every good plan is really a simple one. The more complicated you make it, the more that can go wrong."

"You really plan stuff out, J.C."

"That's my job," he said.

"I guess there's no way. . . ."

"What? What's on your mind, kid?"

"This guy. Monty. He's not, like, one of us, right?"

"One of us? Oh, you mean, he's a square john? Sure. You think they'd let a guy with a record pilot one of those rigs? Monty's a guy who never would have thought of this whole plan on his own. But, some of those citizens, once you figure out how to get their nose open, there's nothing they won't do."

"But what if . . . what if he's like . . . what if he's like Kaiser was?"

"You mean, if he's got some friends waiting around? Not a chance, Eddie. One," he said, ticking off the numbers on his fingers, "like you said, he's not from our world. He wouldn't know where to find a crew could lift that heavy a weight. Two, he don't have a clue where we're staying. He doesn't know anything about this place. All the trust's on us, see?"

"So how does he——?"

"Soon as it's done, he's got to jump. Get gone good. But Monty's slick. He's been planning something like this for years, before we even met him. Just been waiting for the right crew to come along.

"Monty's been making regular trips to New York. There's a plastic surgeon up there that's going to do his face as soon as this is over. He's got a whole new set of ID waiting, too, for when he can get the new pictures taken.

"We know where he's going to hide out until we can get him the money. All he has to do is hold tight for a few days, and then he disappears. They'll never find him."

"I guess. But if he ever does get caught, he'll——"

"Rat us all out, sure. So what? He's never seen you. Besides, if Gus's stuff works like he says, nobody's even going to be *looking* for him, am I right?"

"You're right, J.C.," I said. "You thought of everything."

Gus wanted to play cards that night. Me, him, and J.C., cutthroat hearts. I didn't feel like doing anything with Gus anymore, but I knew I had to.

"I want to play, too," Vonda said. She never had before.

"You can't have betting with four players," Gus said.

"We can play partners," J.C. told him. "Me and Vonda against you and Eddie."

What the fuck's wrong with you?" Gus said to me. "Couldn't you see I was shooting the moon?"

"I'm sorry," I said.

"Get with the program, kid. We're down damn near a hundred bucks already."

"Few weeks from now, you'll be lighting cigars with hundred-dollar bills," J.C. told him.

I knew J.C. and Gus wouldn't be going away anymore. So I wasn't disappointed when Vonda stopped watching my movies with me. She stopped exercising, too.

The only time I saw her was when she came out to the barn one day with J.C. and Gus.

"Hey, what's with the front door on that hearse?" Gus asked me.

"What do you mean?" I said.

"How come it opens from the front? It looks weird."

"They're called 'suicide doors,'" I told him. "They used to make all cars like that."

"I can see why they call them that. Christ, you could fall right out on your face."

"Not if you're careful. And I figure it gives me an extra second or so if I have to get out fast."

"That's why Eddie's the ace," J.C. said. "Best getaway man in the business."

Even with all I knew about him by then, it meant a lot to me, that he said that.

"You're sure he hasn't got a move?" Gus asked J.C. that same night.

"You and Eddie, Jesus Christ," J.C. said. "Monty's got nothing. He's the one's got to trust *us*. He's taking the armored car, but we're taking the money."

Gus didn't say anything.

J.C. took a long deep breath. Then he let it out slow, like he was trying to keep his temper.

"All right," he said, looking at both of us, "one more time. Two men are making the run in the armored car. One of them is Monty. The other guy, the one behind the wheel, he doesn't know anything. We'll be behind those rocks; nobody can see us from the road. When they get close, Monty pulls his piece, makes the other guy drive up to us.

"Monty keeps him under the gun; Gus slips behind him with that pad of chloroform and clamps him down. He goes out like a light, be unconscious for a good hour, minimum.

"When the guy wakes up, he's in the armored car, a few miles away from where we took him. He's cuffed to the steering wheel, but his radio's disabled, and every fuse has been pulled, so his horn and lights don't work.

"Even when the cops finally find him, all he can tell them is that Monty was in on it. He never sees our faces, never hears us talk. But we make *sure* he sees the hearse . . . that's Eddie's job.

"The way the cops dope it out, the robbers and Monty all pile in the hearse to make a getaway. The driver loses control around the curve just opposite the quarry, and it goes over the edge.

"When they finally get down there to examine the wreck, they won't find any actual bodies, just little tiny *pieces* of them, all burned. Even if there's enough left to DNA, none of it's *our* DNA. So even if they don't buy it complete, the only person they can ever look for is Monty.

"And even if they do catch Monty someday, so what? Sure, like Eddie already asked me, he'd rat us out in a heartbeat. But what's he got to tell them? Meanwhile, time's passing, and the statute of limitations is running. This isn't a murder; it's a robbery. Sooner or later, they'll have to throw in the towel."

"Yeah," Gus said. "All Monty's got to do is drive the armored car down the road a few miles, nice and slow, then ditch it and disappear. That'll give us plenty of margin, especially if the base calls him on the radio while he's still behind the wheel."

"And the cops, they'll think we took Monty with us," J.C. said, smiling. "Right over the edge." He turned to look at me. "Hey, Eddie, you sure that ground won't take tracks?"

"Car tracks, just a little, maybe," I said. "But never us, walking back."

"Can't you fix something with the gas pedal, make it go over by itself?" J.C. asked me.

"No. I mean, I *could,* but it might not work. The only way to be sure is to put it in drive, and all three of us shove it over. I've got the idle set up real high. It'll be easy."

"Isn't there something I could do, too?" Vonda said.

"All you have to do is sit right here," J.C. said. "We'll be back with enough money to light you up like a Christmas tree."

Saturday, we all stayed up. When J.C.'s cell phone buzzed, I jumped a little. But it was only Monty, saying that it wasn't going to be that night.

It was a bad week after that. With J.C. and Gus around all the time, Vonda could hardly talk to me. But, sometimes, when no one was looking, she'd give me a quick little secret squeeze.

I spent a lot of time in the barn. But I never watched any of my movies.

*T*he next week was like my first week in prison. It never seemed to get closer to another day.

Saturday night, J.C.'s phone went off again. When he hung up, he said, "It's show time."

We went out to the freezer for the bodies. They were too slippery to handle; we had to wrap them in blankets.

Gus and me loaded the bodies in the back of the hearse. J.C. kept looking at his watch, saying, "Plenty of time, plenty of time."

*W*hen I first poked the nose of the hearse out of the barn, a spring rain was slanting down.

"Roads're going to be greasy," Gus said.

"Eddie knows what he's doing," J.C. told him.

I felt good about what J.C. had said. But Gus was right, and I paid close attention.

I could feel the extra weight in the back right through the wheel. More weight back there helps keep you from sliding, but if the rear end ever does break loose, it makes it harder to catch, too. The trick to driving on wet roads is to stay smooth—it's jerky moves that get you sideways.

J.C. was right about there being plenty of time. When the armored car showed up, we had been waiting in the hearse for over an hour.

We were pretty much hidden behind the big pile of rocks, but I could see the whole road out of the windshield, even with the wipers off. I had my window down, too.

The armored car slowed way down and pulled over. It kept coming, real slow, until it was back in the brush near where we were. Its lights went off.

Two men got out, wearing uniforms. They started walking over toward where we were hiding in the hearse.

When they got close, I could see one man was holding a pistol, aimed at the other one's back.

They stopped not twenty feet from where we were. The one without the gun turned around, so they were facing each other.

I started the engine, so I could pull out and let the armored car driver see us.

"You're crazy if you think you can get away with this," the man without the gun said. "They'll know—"

The shots came so sudden I felt a jolt in my chest. The noise bounced off the rocks like thunder inside a cave. One of the men fell to the ground.

"Fuck!" J.C. said.

Him and Gus ran over to where the man in uniform was standing, still holding his gun. I stayed in the driver's seat.

I heard them saying things to each other. I couldn't make it all out, but I could tell J.C. was mad. He put his palm up like a traffic cop, telling me to keep the hearse where it was.

J.C. held out his hand, and the man in uniform gave over his pistol. J.C. took it, but he didn't point it at anyone, just held it down at his side.

Then J.C. said something, pointing his finger at the man's chest. The man and Gus each took one of the dead man's legs and dragged him over to the hearse. I heard them open the big wide door from the outside, and the thump he made when they heaved him in.

I never turned around. My job was to watch the road. Anyway, I wouldn't have been able to see much with all those bodies piled up in the back.

I saw the man and Gus walk over to where J.C. was waiting. J.C. pointed again. The man in the uniform climbed into the armored car. He drove across to the other side of the road, to where the truck was hidden behind the curtain.

J.C. and Gus walked over on foot. They guided the driver backing up until he was in the right place.

The driver of the armored car got out. Rain beaded on the windshield, but I could see the shapes of three men moving, loading the money into the truck.

It didn't take long. The man in the uniform got back into the armored car, and drove off, heading out the way they had been going at first.

J.C. and Gus ran across the road to the hearse. They jumped in the back and slammed the door behind them.

"Go!" J.C. said to me.

I creeped forward until I was sure it was clear. Then I nailed the gas and we swung out onto the road, heading for the quarry.

It was exactly 1.3 miles away; I had checked it a dozen times. But I'd also sprayed my "X" on a big rock just ahead of it, just to be sure.

When I saw the "X," I hit the brakes to let the rear tires take a set, and spun the wheel to the right. The hearse slid right into the spot where we were supposed to get out and start pushing it.

"Let's move!" J.C. said.

I closed my eyes for a split second. I could see the black car from my dream, coming for me out of the night.

I stomped the gas. The hearse shot forward.

"What the fuck are you—!?" Gus yelled. I could hear him, clawing his way over the bodies to get to me.

I knew it was less than a hundred yards to the edge. I yanked on the cable I had connected to the gas pedal, locking it in place.

The hearse charged into the dark, eating up ground. I was counting to four in my head.

"Eddie!" J.C. screamed.

I felt Gus's hands grabbing for me. I leaned way forward, shoved open the suicide door and dived out. Just like in Vonda's movie.

The back of the hearse flashed past my eyes. The ground came up and smashed me. I thought I was paralyzed for a minute—I couldn't get any breath, but my eyes were wide open.

The hearse went over the edge, engine roaring. I saw the taillights blink red, once.

Breath came into me. I got up, slow. My teeth had gone into my lip, and I was bleeding a little. My left ankle wouldn't take too much weight. But I was okay. Nothing broken.

I looked up and saw I was really close to the edge. I crawled the rest of the way, moving careful because it was so dark.

Just as I looked down, I heard the explosion.

Gus had been right. The blackness below lit up in a giant fireball.

I limped back to the road, feeling a little more strength in the ankle. Then I started back to where we left the truck, cutting through the woods. It was much shorter that way. I knew, because I had practiced.

The truck started right up. I drove the load of money back to the cabin over the back roads. It took a long time, but I kept myself from doing anything stupid.

I did three wide loops around where the cabin was, but nobody was following me. Finally, I drove up and put the truck in the barn. I sat there a minute, listening.

Nothing.

I opened the Thunderbird's trunk. I could see that all the sacks of money from the truck wouldn't fit; we would have to leave some of it. But that was okay; we'd still have enough to last forever.

I limped over to the cabin, sadness and pride swirling together in my chest.

There was only one little light on, in the front window.

I went up the steps and opened the door. Vonda was sitting at the kitchen table. "Eddie," she said.

There was someone over in the corner, standing in a shadow. When he moved, I could see he had a pistol in his hand.

Vonda turned and looked over at him. That's when I knew who he was.

Monty.

Her getaway man.

A NOTE ABOUT THE AUTHOR

ANDREW VACHSS has been a federal investigator in sexually transmitted diseases, a social services caseworker, and a labor organizer, and has directed a maximum-security prison for violent youth. Now a lawyer in private practice, he represents children and youths exclusively. He is the author of numerous novels, including the Burke series, two collections of short stories, and a wide variety of other material, including song lyrics, poetry, graphic novels, and a "children's book for adults." His books have been translated into twenty languages, and his work has appeared in *Parade, Antaeus, Playboy, Esquire, The New York Times,* and numerous other forums. He lives and works in New York City, his native home, and the Pacific Northwest.

The dedicated Web site for Vachss and his work is

www.vachss.com